THE SKY FALLS

LORENZA MAZZETTI

THE SKY FALLS

Translated
from the Italian by
MARGUERITE WALDMAN

DAVID McKAY COMPANY, INC.

NEW YORK

Il Cielo Cade
(Milan, 1961)

The Sky Falls
(London, 1962)

LIBRARY OF CONGRESS CATALOG CARD NUMBER 63-11582

LITHOGRAPHED IN THE UNITED STATES OF AMERICA

NOBLE OFFSET PRINTERS, INC., NEW YORK

To my uncle
WILHELM-ROBERT
EINSTEIN

THEME: Give an account of what you have done today. Development: Today in school the Duce spoke to us and told us to do gymnastics so as to grow strong, well-behaved and ready in case he should call upon us to defend our great Italy, because there's a war on.

I wonder whether it's all right for me to love my sister Baby more than the Duce. Because I love Baby the same as Jesus. Just the same as Jesus, and I love Jesus a little more than God, and God the same as Mussolini, and Italy and the Fatherland less than God but more than my yellow bear.

After I had handed in my composition exercise-book I began looking at the photograph of the Duce on the cover of my exercise-book with the multiplication table. On the back was a photograph of the King, His Majesty Victor Emmanuel III, King of Italy. I concentrated my gaze on the Duce. I stared him in the eye to make sure that I was right:

Yes, the Duce is good.

He appears in various aspects, full face, profile, once in a helmet, once in a laurel wreath like an ancient Roman. In the exercise-book the Duce appears stripped to the waist, among peasants mowing grain. In another one there's the

Duce surrounded by many children dressed as Sons of the Wolf and as Little Daughters of Italy like me. His gaze is kind and intense like the gaze of Jesus among the children in the 'religion' textbook.

The Duce also hangs above the head of the Signora, our teacher, and under him is the crucifix. Then there are the Duce and the Führer, both of them in profile, smiling at each other. The Führer is the head of Germany and the Duce's friend. I too should like to be the Duce's friend.

The girl on the bench beside me smells of cheese. My little sister, Baby, is in a different form. She does not smell of cheese nor of sheep. Neither do I, who am called Penny, smell of cheese, but when I play with Pasquetta, Pierino, Zeffirino and Lea I smell of the stable too. Pasquetta, the girl on the bench beside me, when she eats her mamma's sandwiches, often smells of salami too, but she has another odour, the permanent one, which is entirely her own. All the children smell of hay and of sheep.

The teacher said that for tomorrow we were to take as a composition subject our dreams in the night. 'Describe what you dreamed last night.'

'What did you dream, Penny?' Lea asked me.

'Leave me alone, goose.'

Lea began to giggle because she read something in my notebook that made her laugh. I have no idea what.

My foreign name among so many names like Pierino, Pierino the first, Pierino the second, sound odd. With my starched white apron, polished shoes, my legs, neck and ears clean, amongst so many children who smell of the stables, I feel like a white kangaroo.

Lea rose to her feet.

'Teacher! Penny dreamed the Madonna was bald!'

'The Madonna bald? What are you talking about? Sit down and keep quiet.'

Lea stopped laughing.

'The Madonna is not bald,' stated the teacher. She had me bring my exercise-book and drew a large red mark across it. Her face was red too.

I burst into sobs. The Signora frightened me because she was so red and perspiring and was looking hard at me.

'But I dreamed it.'

'Be quiet!'

'It's true, it's true, I dreamed it!'

She gave me two smart slaps and sent me into the corner with my face to the wall. Then she told the priest about it.

'The Devil is in this little girl's home,' said the priest. 'We must help her, we must try and prevent her and her relatives from going to hell. Penny can save herself, but what about her uncle? He is condemned to eternal torment. Do you believe in God, Penny?'

'Me, yes.'

'But your relatives . . . and your uncle . . .' he bent over me, 'he doesn't believe in Him, he never sends you to Mass. Whoever does not believe in God is in the hands of Satan.'

[9]

It seems to me, in thinking my uncle over, that every now and then when he scolds me the Devil is inside him.

'We must save them, we must save these two children and their relatives.'

The priest said that my uncle's soul was in danger because he was a Jew, that is to say he did not believe in Jesus, and that the Jews had killed Jesus. To save him it was necessary to offer up 'little flowers'. Every little self-denial, however small, was of value. With many penances and sacrifices it was possible to obtain a place at least in purgatory for my uncle, who was condemned to everlasting fire. Then the priest dwelt upon the various sufferings which the people in hell are obliged to undergo. So much so that I wondered how the damned manage not to die of all those punishments.

'Is it true that they walk on beans with their feet cut?' asked Zeffirino.

From hell the priest went on to speak of the various forms of torture that exist.

The school-bell rang and we sang 'Giovinezza'. And then 'The Piave'. The Signora does not like us to shout the national anthems nor to finish them with 'boom boom'. But we shouted, 'The Piave murmured low, "The stranger shall not pass!" Boom boom!'

I wonder why it is that the Duce's head is so nice and shiny and hairless, but I prefer not to ask the teacher, on account of the bald Madonna I dreamed of who, now that

I come to think of it, resembles the Duce. The Duce has, in fact, a halo about his head, like a saint.

The song I like best is the song of the Little Daughters of Italy:

> *We are the golden dawn,*
> *Gaily we grow in the air and the sunlight,*
> *We are the daughters of Italy,*
> *Desiring to make Italy greater still.*

> *Our tiny hearts,*
> *Tiny but ardent with love,*
> *Like small warbling birds pray to God:*
> *Save the Duce evermore.*

WHEN school was over Baby and I stood outside, in the janitor's care, waiting for the car to fetch us and bring us up to the Villa. Because of the absence of cars in the region and the presence of the chauffeur everybody looked at us. The chauffeur lifted us into the De Soto, then closed the doors and started the motor. None of the boys and girls could resist waving when the car started. They looked down the country road after it until it disappeared up a steep slope towards the hilltop. The passers-by stood aside and removed their caps at its passage, respectfully.

Baby and I have not lived long at the Villa. The chauffeur brought us here in the big De Soto which is a car all velvet on the inside. Uncle Wilhelm's chauffeur has gold buttons and a cap and sidewhiskers and is called Cosimo and he is also butler at the Villa.

Baby and I feel almost as much in awe of Cosimo as of Uncle. Baby and I had never seen Uncle; Papa had told us about him, but now Papa is no longer here, nor Mamma either. They are in heaven. From up there they look down to see if Baby and I are good, obedient and respectful as they want us to be. They're up there especially to see whether we two are good.

The chauffeur says that Baby and I are two poor little

orphans and he's sorry for us, I don't know exactly why. But I like it when people say 'poor little thing' and stroke my hair.

Of course since Mamma and Papa went up to heaven nobody kisses us before we go to sleep at night and when we wake up in the morning; it will be like this until they return from heaven. When, I don't know.

Our uncle's estate is very large and it takes Uncle Wilhelm a year on horseback to get round it. Every day he goes on horseback to see a peasant and asks him, 'How are you? How are the crops?' and they take off their caps and say, 'Thank you, Sir.'

Baby and I, when we arrived up here for the first time, made a curtsey to Aunt Katchen, Papa's sister, who kissed us, and so did Marie. But Annie, who is two years older than me, is jealous of our coming—that's what Elsa the cook says—and does not want Aunty and Uncle to love us better than her.

For this reason, as soon as we went into the garden to play with the rocking-horse and the other toys, Annie said no, that the toys were hers.

Then Baby and I pulled her pigtails, because she was kicking and hitting us.

Annie began to scream so loudly that Uncle came out and said, 'You naughty girl, Penny, why do you pull Annie's hair?' Annie went on crying and Uncle punished us because it isn't right for two of us to strike Annie who is alone against us

[13]

both, poor little thing, and he spoke to us of 'Justice'.

I cried a great deal and then I went to Elsa for consolation between her knees, and so did Baby. Elsa smells of onion and her little chain with the cross hangs between her two breasts when she bends over to kiss me and it seems to me that between the two breasts there's a tunnel where I'd like to stay in the warm while she sings 'Ave Maria' and her voice rises up to heaven.

Elsa washes us, combs our hair, ties our white aprons on, and our big starched sky-blue ribbons, and we smell of fresh linen. What a bore Elsa is when she wants at all costs to wash my neck, nose and ears. Baby yells. At my age I can wash by myself but she insists that my neck is dirty. Then I say, 'Where is it dirty, Elsa? Show me where.'

And then we get into the big car and the chauffeur brings us down the steep road to the school in the village called Rosa Maltoni, like the Duce's mother.

The teacher received us very kindly, and said that all the children should be nice to us because Baby and I had no mamma or papa.

UNCLE was playing chess with Aunt Katchen. Aunt Katchen is Protestant and Marie and Annie also believe in God and in Jesus and are Protestant. But they don't go to Mass because Uncle does not wish it, because he's not Christian; he is Jewish, that is, he does not believe in Jesus.

When they play chess they sit face to face for hours looking very serious. I'm always terrified of my uncle just because he is so serious, and he often frightens me when he's angry with me. It sometimes happens that he won't speak to me for days on end. My great joy is when Uncle is willing to play chess with me.

Elsa washed our hands and said to us, 'Whatever do you do with the ink? Do you drink it?'

At table Uncle spoke at length, about business I think, because they all spoke German, the grown-ups. There were guests at the table in addition to Edith and Arthur and their Pekinese. Aunt Katchen was giving us French and English lessons and on this account we called her Aunty in English. When she turned to us she always spoke French or English, and this was a bore because one had to answer her in the same language whereas I was dying to go and sit in the rocking-chair. But Annie always got there first.

At the table all three of us would fidget on our chairs until Uncle said we could leave. Then we'd jump up and dash for the rocking-chair. When this happened, a plate would often drop to the floor.

Marie asked me why my eyes were red. I told her my eyes were red because I had dreamed the Madonna was bald. I felt sad when I saw my uncle and all the others and even Aunty burst out laughing. They all laughed and looked at me and said, 'The Madonna bald!' and burst out laughing all over again. Aunty repeated the words in French and German and they had to slap her on the back because she couldn't stop laughing and nearly choked.

I am more and more convinced that the Devil is in the Villa. They have all got to be saved. Marie and Annie and the rest.

Marie was learning the violin and so was Annie.

I love Marie, but I don't like Annie because she isn't nice to Baby and me; still I don't wish her to go to hell. According to the way she happens to be feeling, Annie plays with Baby and me or puts on Marie's high heels and pretends to be a lady. Even so, she continues to keep her toys to herself and not let us touch them. Annie is remarkably strong too, and Baby and I are not able to stand up to her when she comes and steals our pine-nuts.

But Marie is good. Her schoolmates often come to see her and play tennis with her. Of all her friends the one I like best is Leonardo. Partly because he sometimes plays ping-pong with me. I often pick flowers for Marie, who sees to putting them in the drawing-room and the guests' rooms. Marie is good, I don't want her to go to hell. But she doesn't know that and bears me a grudge because I broke the china lamp on her writing table.

'Go away, naughty little beast!' she screamed at me, bending down to pick up the pieces.

'But I didn't do it on purpose.'

'You and Baby always break everything.'

'Don't talk like that.' And I started gathering the bits of china. They were pretty eighteenth-century ladies dancing a minuet around the lamp.

'Naughty,' said Marie.

'Everybody scolds me in this house. Nobody knows how much I love you . . .' I said, on the way to the door. 'If I were a man I'd marry you.'

Only Jesus and the Madonna know that I'm not bad at heart. But if God knows everything I wonder if He knows who there was before God.

And then there's Signor Pit who teaches Annie and Marie to play the violin. Marie is the better and already plays Corelli, whereas Annie always plays wrong and only just managed to learn 'Oh Tannenbaum' and 'Stille Nacht' in time for Christmas.

That evening Signor Pit asked Aunt Katchen if she would dance.

Signor Pit lifted her off her feet and began dancing round with her, making her pirouette to the right and to the left like a doll. I think he must be a little in love.

Signor Pit always dresses badly in spite of being rich, and instead of a belt to hold up his trousers he wears a piece of string. Often he does not even bother to button his trousers. Aunt Katchen says he never washes, but my uncle says he is an eccentric who plays the piano very well. Signor Pit has a passion for our Angora cat whose name is Giovanni, and takes long walks with him. He keeps talking to him all the time. We eavesdrop and listen to what he says. He can't easily see us because he is nearsighted and we hide in the bushes saying, 'Miaow! Miaow!' and pretending to be the cat.

In addition to playing the piano and whistling while he plays as though he were a violin, Signor Pit is a rock-climber. He goes for walks early in the morning, dressed for climbing the Alps. In his room we've found so many sweets. Horrid man! He's never given us a single one. In revenge I play tricks on him. For instance I put them all in my mouth and then I put them back on his dressing table. He too plays chess with my uncle, and when he loses he shuts himself in his room and does not come down for lunch or dinner. Uncle sends his dinner to his room but he refuses to open the door and eats sweets.

[18]

One evening, while we were all in the drawing-room listening to a concert, Signor Pit rushed down the stairs and into the room with a red face and his eyes popping out with rage.

'*Genug! Genug!*' he cried to the astonishment of all. And he hurled himself upon the radio, snapping it off and showering blows on it with his fists.

'But Signor Pit!'

'Dat make me seeck!' and he sat down at the piano and started playing the piece that had been on the radio. Nobody spoke. Signor Pit is Uncle's friend and is allowed to do anything, even to come to table with dirty hands. I am jealous of him.

Signor Pit played and played. His hands ran up and down the keyboard. Everybody listened.

Signor Pit stopped for an instant and hurled his stiff collar and tie on to the ground. Then he continued playing. The house was full of notes. Signor Pit struck the piano with his swift fingers as though he wanted to vent his feelings on it. He stopped for a moment and threw his jacket on the ground and again started playing furiously, biting his lips and making dreadful faces. Everybody listened in ecstasy. But I was waiting for him to take off his cuffs and waistcoat. A moment later his cuffs flew over our heads and hit Signor Arthur, who raised his hands to his head.

After other frantic blows on the keyboard Signor Pit ended the concert and stood up.

[19]

'*Wunderbar!*' said my uncle. The others applauded while Baby and I collected Signor Pit's clothing scattered about the room and brought it back to him.

OUR cook Elsa and Cosimo and Rosa the housemaid always go to Mass on Sundays. At the Villa there's a private chapel, and the priest comes to say Mass. All the peasants come, but our uncle doesn't, nor does he send us.

Rosa makes love with Nello, the peasant, and Pierino's mamma says that Nello has made a baby for her by kissing her. Rosa wears perfume on Sundays and smells of onion the other days. On Sundays she stands before the mirror getting ready to go out, and Baby and I look at her. She says:

'Jesus Christ, how fat I am!'

Our uncle doesn't want us always to be with Rosa or the peasants' children because he says we'll end by speaking like they do. But Baby and I go with them anyhow, in secret. Rosa has a bright pink dress and then when she's all white with powder so that you can't recognize her, she starts to leave. Then she comes running back to the mirror to see whether everything is in order. After she has stared at herself for half an hour she gets a silly look on her face.

'Rosa, why do you look at yourself?'

She tells me to be quiet, but she always listens to my advice. Then I take the comb and I comb her hair, and so does Baby and we curl it to make her look pretty.

'Holy Mary, is the dress too tight?' she asks me. 'How about this rose? Shall I wear it here on my breast, Penny?'

'Higher up.' Rosa pins it higher.

'Lower down.' Rosa pins it lower.

As she does so she looks at her stomach.

'Men are swine.'

'What?'

'All swine, including Mussolini.' She goes out slamming the door.

I love Rosa but I won't have her speak like that of the Duce. It's Nello who puts those ideas into her head, I know it. I'll kill Rosa if I hear her speaking ill again of Benito Mussolini.

Baby and I are always living up in the trees with the peasants' children, Lea, Pasquetta, Zeffirino, Pierino. Behind the Villa there's a dense wood of old laurels. Most of the time we're up in the branches doing 'the throw'.

'The throw' means you throw yourself from one branch to another and then do the 'caperswing': that's when you hoist yourself up with a jump to a third branch, from which you dangle head downward holding on by your feet and knees.

Once Baby fell and hurt her back. What a scare! She was crying.

'Does it hurt, Baby? I'll give you all my pine-cones if you stop crying.'

[22]

Pasquetta brought fresh water and we made her poultices of wet sand and leaves.

Every day Leonardo comes. He lives on another hilltop nearby. He always arrives on horseback. I asked him whether he knew how to climb trees but he said no. So I brought him to the laurels and said I would show him 'the throw'. I did all my favourite things for him, made 'caperswings' and dangled from the branches by my feet, with my head downward. I also did 'the angel', spreading out my arms like wings and swinging head downward. Leonardo tried it too.

'What are you doing up there?' asked Marie, who was looking for him. 'Come and have tea.'

Leonardo went away to the Villa and I stayed in the tree thinking how much I loved him.

Sometimes I keep out of the way when he comes, because I've been naughty and as a punishment I have to wear a paper band around my head with 'méchante' or 'paresseuse' or 'menteuse' written on it. If I don't study my French or English Aunty makes me wear the 'chapeau d'âne' and I feel ashamed and stay in the medlar tree.

So there's Uncle Wilhelm, Aunt Katchen and also Marie and Annie to be saved, to say nothing of the guests and their Pekinese. And there's Baby and me to be saved as well.

Baby didn't yet know there was the Devil in our house. She had to be told. And what if there's the Devil in Baby too? I turned sharply and thought I detected the Devil in Baby's eyes. I've got to tell her.

Baby was standing under the large oak and stooping to chase a dragon-fly.

'Look Penny! A dragon-fly!'

'It's a grasshopper.'

Baby stooped to look at the grasshopper. I stooped to look at Baby. Supposing the Devil were in Baby too? I turned suddenly and thought I detected the Devil in Baby's eyes. I told her so. Then we turned and stood back to back and counted, 'One! two! three!' and we sprang round and looked each other in the eye. Baby stared at me glassily without batting an eyelash. I grew scared and began shouting, 'Baby! Baby! Answer me!'

But Baby stared at me more and more glassily.

'Baby!' I shouted, beginning to shake her very hard. Baby remained quite lifeless and let herself be shaken as she gazed blankly ahead of her. I tried to make her laugh but she stared at me with the eyes of the Devil. Then I began to weep with fright. There was Baby in front of me with the Devil inside her.

'You're the Devil! You're the Devil!'

Then Baby began skipping about all over the place smiling broad smiles to reassure me.

'Penny, I swear to you I'm not the Devil!'

'Cross your heart?'

'Yes Penny, I swear it. I'm not the Devil, and you, aren't you either?' asked Baby, looking me in the eye.

I told Baby that the priest had said the Devil was in possession of our uncle and that to save him it would be necessary to offer up 'little flowers'. The priest says that every little self-denial, even the smallest, has a value and that with many self-denials and sacrifices perhaps we shall succeed in keeping our uncle out of hell. The priest says that in hell there's real fire, which really burns; and forever, too.

'It never stops?'

'Never.'

'What does never mean?'

'Never means always. The priest says there's not only the eternal fire but there are so many other sufferings as well. He says some devils make the damned walk on beans after cutting the soles of their feet.'

I remembered his words perfectly, and all the details. The priest described the water torture. He says another way of making people die is to spread salt on them and then send the goats to lick the tips of their toes till they're tickled to death.

At table Baby asked Uncle whether it were really possible to be tickled to death. Uncle said yes and told us that a famous writer called Aretino had in fact died of laughing.

After lunch we went into the garden.

'How will Uncle die?'

'I don't know . . . Uncle won't die.'

'No,' said Baby, 'he won't go to hell . . . I'll go in his place.'

'That's impossible.'

'Then *you* go.'

'It's impossible because there's the Last Judgement.'

Baby was distressed. 'But if we make sacrifices and offer "little flowers" will he go to hell?' she asked.

'No.'

'Then Uncle won't die in the eternal fire?'

'No. He won't die.'

'WHAT penance shall we do?'

'Let's see who can stand on one foot the longest.'

'That's no penance. We've got to suffer.'

'What can we do to suffer?'

'We must do like the little martyrs.'

'Let's cross this field of thorns over and over until we bleed.'

Lea, Pierino and Zeffirino looked at the field; it was full of dried-up yellow flowers with thorns instead of leaves.

I flung myself into the field at a gallop but stopped half-way across because of the pain. The others had not yet budged.

'Come on,' I shouted, and began to run, with tears of pain streaming from my eyes. In order to feel it less I advanced in leaps. I stopped at the far side of the field, writhing with pain. The others had reached the middle. They were standing still and had not the courage to go forward or back. There were nettles, too, as well as brambles. I looked at my legs. They were all red, and they burned. The others were coming nearer, leaping and squealing.

At last they arrived, first one, then another.

'Ouch, ouch!' and they rolled on the ground.

Afterwards Baby arrived, last of all.

I looked at Baby's legs. They were all red, with a lot of little prickles still attached to them. Pasquetta, too, raised her frock above her thighs and showed us her legs: 'Look!'

Lea was twitching all over.

'That's enough!' and she put moist leaves on her thighs and the calves of her legs to ease the pain.

'No, it's not. We said we'd cross the field ten times and we've only done it once.' And I began to run, followed by the others.

The thorns entered our flesh. We all started together at the word, 'Go!' yelling like savages to spur ourselves on. The real pain began afterwards and was caused by the nettles.

Towards sundown Uncle appeared on the hill, accompanied by his guests. He called, 'It's late! Penny, Baby, come home!' And he waved at us. He moved towards the Villa with the others. His head with its white hair! I feel that I love him. I looked at my legs full of red spots and wiped away the trickling blood with laurel leaves. Then I wiped Baby's legs with other laurel leaves. Baby cried and to make her stop I picked two or three arbutus berries and gave them to her.

'I didn't cross the field,' said Baby.

As a matter of fact when she had reached the middle she had been stuck there, incapable of moving either forward or back.

'But you're little.'

It was growing dark and Zeffirino said, 'I'm going home, else I'll cop it.'

In fact Zeffirino's dad could be heard shouting, 'Zeffirinooo! If you don't come home right this minute I'll see to you properly, you rascal! And there's the water to be fetched.'

Zeffirino's dad takes off his belt when he's angry and runs after him shouting and lashing out at him. Lea's and Pierino's mamma smacks them too if they don't do their work; and if they run away and won't let themselves be caught she takes off her clogs and throws them at them.

Oh, how I wish Uncle would whip me with his belt and give me smacks instead of looking at me with that air of disapproval and refusing to speak to me or smile at me for days at a time.

The maids called us to give us our baths and send us to supper. After supper they sent us to bed.

Annie can stay up ten minutes longer than we two because she's bigger, and so she sits in the rocking-chair and looks at us condescendingly. We kiss Uncle, Aunt Katchen and Marie on the cheek. We make a curtsey to the guests.

Often when I've been naughty and come to Uncle to give him a goodnight kiss he draws his face away with a reproachful air.

That evening Annie was sitting in the rocking-chair and tripped me up, so I jumped on her, partly in envy, partly in

[29]

rage, and pulled her plaits. My uncle, seeing this, made me fill in ten pages in my punishment notebook the following day, with the sentence, 'I must not pull plaits.'

I turned the pages of the notebook. It was nearly finished. It was full of sentences like this: 'I must not tell lies.' 'I must not throw cups or glasses at people's heads.' 'I must not use the scissors to cut up dresses I dislike.' 'I must be polite, obedient and respectful.' 'I must not answer back when I am rebuked.' 'It is wrong to speak at table with one's mouth full.' 'It is wrong to peek through keyholes.' 'It is wrong to trip up the housemaids.' 'It is wrong to trample on the grain in the fields.' 'It is wrong to soil the walls with pictures or with dirty hands.' 'It is wrong to throw stones and break windows.' 'One does not live in the trees.' 'One does not speak loudly.' 'One does not sing Fascist songs when Uncle is asleep.' 'One does not play with the peasants' children.' 'One is not familiar with the servants.' 'It is wrong to go to bed with one's clothes on.'

THE grown-ups were playing cricket. You could hear them laughing. Auntie was sitting in a deckchair in the shade of a mulberry tree, reading *Vol de Nuit*.

Uncle had his gold-handled cane beside him. Edith was painting a tree; her husband, Arthur, sat beside her smoking a pipe. They came from a neighbouring villa and thought much less of us little ones than of their Pekinese, Cipi, who was treated like a king and bit me whenever I came near him.

Then there were the guests, an old gentleman, large and stout with a red moustache and eyeglasses, who was called Van Marle and worked at art history. He lived on the other side of the mountain. He spent many hours with Uncle in the study full of books.

When he arrived with his car he drew up at the foot of the flight of steps to the Villa and stopped a minute to play hop-scotch with us. You make marks on the ground with chalk and then you hop on one leg only. Signor Van Marle tried but he never won. He is so big and fat and always ends by putting down the other foot too; then Baby laughs and shouts.

Cosimo, the butler, came to call him and tell him that tea was ready and took him away, to Baby's and my fury. Annie followed Signor Van Marle into the drawing-room, not forgetting to turn round and make a face at us.

Edith was painting the tree. Edith did not like us looking at her while she painted. So we had to roost at the top of a nearby tree in absolute silence and terribly uncomfortable positions the whole time she was painting, in order to see how you do a tree.

We knew at what hour she came with her easel and her Pekinese, and would lie in wait for her. I would look at the sky between the branches and came to recognize various birdcalls. Lea could actually imitate them.

'I've got to do pipi,' said Baby, taken by surprise.

'Hold it in.'

'The little fool, she's got to do pipi.' By laughing Pasquetta made the branch creak.

From our vantage point we could see Edith, the canvas and the landscape which she kept erasing continually.

'I can't wait,' said Baby and did pipi.

Signora Edith was deeply offended and never spoke to us again.

'I feel much better, I thought I was going to burst.'

'Half-wit.'

'Half-wit yourself.'

'Monkey-face!'

'Monkey-face yourself!' said Baby crying, and ran away. I was distressed.

[32]

'Leave her alone!' cried Pasquetta when I called her back.

'No, no!' I began to run. I could put up with anything except not having Baby smile at me. If Baby is angry with me it's as though the sky were to grow dark and the sun turn black and my heart were slowly freezing up.

'Baby! Baby!' I shouted running after her through the fields. 'Come here, give me a kiss! Just one!'

Baby continued to run through the grass. 'No,' she said.

'Just one little one, Baby!'

She stopped, out of breath.

'All right,' and she gave me a moist kiss on the cheek. Then we rolled down the green slope hugging each other. The others arrived and rolled down too, through the green grass. I was hugging Baby very tight and thinking that I was called Penny and Baby Baby, and that she was not Penny. How does it happen that I'm Penny and not Baby? And how would I be if I were Baby?

'Baby, doesn't it seem strange to you that you aren't me?'

'What?'

'I love you so much that it doesn't seem possible that you aren't me. I don't know what you are and you don't know what I am.'

'You're Penny.'

[33]

'I feel as if I were this tree, and you, what do you feel as if you were?'

Baby said she felt like that cricket who was singing, and I said I felt like that swallow, and we went on this way for quite a while.

'WHAT do you want?' The priest glowered at Zeffirino, who was waving his hand in the air.

'Father, please may I go . . .'

'No, not now.'

Then he went on and said that Pasquetta and Lea and all the others were to learn the catechism so they could be confirmed, and that they were to teach it to us too, in secret, instead of playing.

'Consider the great evil we commit when we give offence to God, our Lord and Father, who has heaped us with blessings, loves us dearly, and infinitely deserves to be loved above all other things and served with all faithfulness . . . You again? What do you want?'

'I can't wait.'

'Go and come back at once.'

Zeffirino slipped out of the classroom.

'Remember that the Passion of Our Lord Jesus Christ was caused by our sins, and that because of us He was scourged, beaten until He bled; the soldiers took away His clothing and cast dice for His tunic. They brought Him before Pontius Pilate and said, "Shall we crucify Him or Barabbas?"'

'And what do you think Pontius Pilate replied? Barabbas?

No! Pontius Pilate had water brought and washed his hands. What would you have done in Pilate's place? Would you have had Jesus, the Son of God, crucified? Answer me that.'

He pointed his finger at us awaiting a reply from the class.

'No!' I cried, leaping to my feet.

'You wouldn't?' said the priest wrathfully. 'Even Peter, one of the Apostles themselves, said to Jesus, "I will never betray thee", and then he denied Him thrice on the night of the Crucifixion. And thrice the cock crowed.

'Silence!' he warned the class, 'don't make so much noise, else I'll straighten you out.'

He joined his hands and told us to repeat after him, 'My most merciful Saviour, I have sinned, and greatly sinned, against Thee by my fault, by my most grievous fault . . .'

We all said it after him in chorus.

'. . . rebelling against Thy holy Law and preferring my whims to Thee, my God and Heavenly Father.'

I did not clearly understand these words; I sought in vain for a sin of mine but could not find any. So I felt ashamed. Finally I thought of one: not following the priest when he prayed and letting my mind wander to our games in the fields, with Baby and the others, to the crickets, which are green when they're born and are like maggots for fishbait before they come out of their shells. Then they sit in the sun and I watch them and after half an hour they

[36]

turn from green to black and sing if Lea tickles them on the tummy. Lea does not know that you can die of laughing.

We repeated in chorus:

'Behold O kind and most sweet Jesus, I cast myself on my knees in Thy sight, and with most fervent desire of soul I beseech Thee to impress upon my heart lively sentiments of faith, hope and charity, with true repentance for my sins and a firm purpose of amendment, while with deep affection and grief I contemplate Thy five most precious wounds'. Here the priest turned to us and, pointing his finger, cried, 'It's your fault that Christ died on the Cross! Died for us! To wash away our sins, do you understand?'

He raised his voice: 'On the Day of Judgement He will return and then we'll see who gets into Paradise! And don't you go imagining that it's comfortable in Hell. It's full of devils there and if you don't do good works now it'll be too late afterwards. And therefore even if you've only got a speck as tiny as this . . .'—he denoted a dot between his fingers—'. . . it'll show plain as a pikestaff on the Day of Judgement!'

9

WHEN I came into the drawing-room they were all sitting round the table waiting for us. On the tea-cloth stood a magnificent tray of cream buns which immediately made my mouth water.

'Oh, here she is at last!' exclaimed my aunt. 'What have you been doing? Why is your face all black? Where's Baby?'

'Oh, just near by in the laurel grove,' I replied, sitting down at the table.

'What's she doing?'

'We tied her up because we're having a war.'

But my aunt and uncle leapt to their feet. It was beginning to rain.

'We were playing this game and that's why we had to tie her and we painted our faces black because we're Abyssinians. Pierino was the Duce on horseback. Baby wanted to be the Hero dressed as a Little Daughter of Italy.'

My aunt said that Baby was afraid of thunder and that she'd certainly take ill and other exaggerations like that just because of a little cold and a little rain.

It infuriated me to see the house upside down and my uncle angry for a matter of no importance. The most maddening part of it was that I couldn't eat the cream buns because I had to go and bring the whole family to Baby who was perfectly happy to be the Hero dressed as a Little Daughter of Italy.

It was terrible what Uncle said to me and the others repeated. They said I was disobedient, spiteful and a heartless little liar. And I, who got all wet going out and fetching Baby, had neither sympathy nor cream buns like her. I was sent to my room, like a dog.

It was shameful to hear them all. The things they said about me were terrible, as if I couldn't hear. Always my fault and never Baby's because Baby is smaller.

My uncle is for justice. My uncle is justice in person. Has all justice got on the inside of my uncle? What about justice being a woman?

Sent to my bedroom like a dog. And Baby eating the cream buns!

Now Uncle is knocking at the door. He wants to know if I'm sorry. I do not reply. I am not sorry because I'm not to blame. But Uncle will never understand because of the bad habit he has of always telling the truth and of having justice inside him.

Uncle's knocking but I don't reply. I hide my head under the sheet. No, I am not naughty, no, I am not a wretch, no, I am not thankless; I don't answer. And what if Uncle knocks the door down?

'Penny, answer me.'

I come out from under the sheet and shout, 'No,

I won't ask to be forgiven, I'm not naughty, I'm not naughty!'

My uncle goes away, giving orders to Marie not to let me out until I have written a hundred times: 'It is wrong to answer back when grown people reprimand us.'

The grown-ups, the grown-ups. The grown-ups are always right and there's nothing we children can do about it: my truth and my lies aren't real.

But I believe in my lies and I believe, I believe absolutely, that I'm good and that I've never done anything bad, and I want to show Uncle that I love him.

But what can I do to show him that? To think that I'd give my life for him and he doesn't even know it!

Baby said too that she'd give her life for Uncle, and also her soul.

But Uncle said that he'd rather we were good, obedient and respectful. Oh how I wish my uncle would strike me rather than bear me a grudge for so long!

Uncle returned a number of times but I was still shut inside my room and did not wish to repent.

Late in the afternoon, seeing Baby playing in the garden, and feeling hungry, I suddenly ran down the front staircase shouting, 'I'm sorry! I'm sorry! I've been naughty!'

Elsa made me a sandwich with ham and one with cheese and I went out to look for Baby. When she saw me Baby gave me a big smile and some pine-nuts that she was crushing. It had stopped raining and the snails had come out. We began watching the snails and Pierino gathered some to be purged and eaten.

To satisfy my uncle I pretended I had been naughty and was sorry. Uncle says we'll begin all over again and that it's not really such a difficult thing to be good, at least for a few days.

10

WE met every day under the large oak.

'To what end has God created us?'

'God has created us to know Him, love Him and serve Him in this world and to be happy with Him forever in heaven.'

'What is heaven?'

'Heaven is eternal enjoyment of God; it is our enjoyment, in Him, of our happiness, and of every other good, without any evil.'

'I don't understand,' wailed Baby.

'She never understands anything, Baby, she wastes all our time, that's what she does. Goodness, she can't ever keep still for a second, always watching the ants; naturally if you don't listen you'll never understand,' said Pasquetta.

'The flies are stinging me,' said Baby.

'I'll sting you if you don't sit still and listen. Penny, you explain it to Baby, it's so simple . . . it means that God is in heaven and we'll go up there to Him to love Him, serve Him and be happy with Him. What's so hard to understand about that, can *you* see?'

'Let's get on with it,' said Pierino.

His feet, as I lay stretched on my stomach in the grass, came close to my face. They smelled of hay.

'And who goes to heaven?'

Lea and Pasquetta replied in chorus, 'Those who deserve heaven are the good, that is, those who love and faithfully serve God, and die in His grace. The wicked, who do not serve God and die in mortal sin, deserve hell.'

The chorus stopped.

'But why is Uncle wicked?' demanded Baby.

'The Master is wicked because he's not baptized and is a Jew,' said Zeffirino.

'The priest said so,' Lea added.

'My uncle is good,' Baby insisted.

'Uncle is good,' I repeated.

'No, the Master is not baptized and Original Sin is wiped out only by holy Baptism, therefore he is a sinner.'

'And what is Original Sin?' asked Baby, more and more plaintive and resentful.

'Original Sin is the sin humanity committed . . . committed . . .' Pasquetta did not remember how to go on. Lea continued, speaking all in one breath. '. . . which humanity committed in Adam its head and which through Adam each man contracts by natural descent.'

Then she added, 'And since among the children of Adam only the Holy Virgin was preserved, we should pray to the Virgin who is without sin, pure as pure . . . Don't you see what a saintly face she has?'

We all looked at the picture of the Madonna on the book.

'What rosy lips! And she's got two eyes like two drops of dew,' said Lea.

'She's got a snake under her foot!'

'Yes, but the snake can't do anything at all to the Madonna; can't you see how she's crushing him with her foot?'

'The snake is the Devil trying to tempt her.'

'Yes, but Uncle is good and will go to heaven,' said Baby.

'No, the Master—that's what the priest said too—he's a foreigner and he'll go to hell, because the Jews don't believe in Jesus or Our Blessed Lady.'

'It's not true, Uncle Wilhelm will not go to hell.'

'Oh yes he will,' said Pasquetta. 'Besides, he never goes to Mass, neither him nor the others, and he never sends you either, and he doesn't teach you the catechism and if it wasn't for us teaching you you'd go to hell too, the both of you.'

''s true,' said Zeffirino looking solemn.

'I'm scared,' said Baby, bursting into tears.

Pierino said, ''tisn't true, not them, the priest said it himself, because they were baptized before their mamma died.'

'Don't you remember your mamma?'

'No,' said Baby.

'And you, Penny? Do you?'

'No,' I said, trying to force my memory. But my first

memory was Baby. Baby and me on a terrace and swallows in the sky. I know it was at the Piazza di Spagna and that the concierge was called Rosina. That's where we were born. That's where Papa worked as a director. When I was small we lived there and my only memories are the terrace, the roofs, the swallows and the noise of the motor-cars. The house was empty and I remember only Baby. Papa was always being a director and the German Fräulein locked us in and left our food on the table. If we did not like it we hid it under the cushions of the armchairs. The Fräulein was young and pretty and her name was Lucy. Once Baby and I climbed up the green trellises with wistaria twined round and round them. We climbed high up and were looking at an old man who, from the window opposite, was making signs to us and shaking his head with a very serious expression, as if he were saying, 'No'. To see him better we kept climbing higher and higher leaning forward and waving to him. Suddenly the door behind us opened and lots of people came out on to the terrace and, with the friendliest smiles, asked us to come down. When we did come down I was mortified, and so was Baby, to be given all those smacks, and we began to cry.

'But did nobody ever bring you to Mass?' asked Zeffirino.

My father arrived with a large doll, so big that we were frightened of it, and put us in the car and left us with a friend of his, a painter called Ugo and his wife Renata, who had three children and they all hugged and kissed us. Renata was the first to speak to us of Jesus.

One day Renata took us on a train and left us here at the Villa with Papa's sister Katchen and Uncle Wilhelm because Papa had gone to heaven to Mamma in the car.

Uncle never takes us in his arms, Annie is mean to us and Aunty gives us hours of dreadful English and German lessons in the shade of the ilex with the crickets singing loudly and Lea and Zeffirino peeping out from the bushes.

Renata said to us, 'Be good and don't annoy your uncle,' and then disappeared.

'They don't seem to teach you a thing at home. Don't they even tell you about Adam and Eve?'

'No,' said Baby, 'not even about Adam and Eve.'

One day Renata gave us a prayer book which did have a picture of Adam and Eve and of the Angel Gabriel with the flaming sword. She gave it to us before we went to the Villa, and she told us Uncle was so rich and that it was better for us to be at the Villa, but she said to remember her and Jesus and the Angel Gabriel and little St. John.

'Do you at least know how many sins there are?'

'No,' said Baby.

'Original sin, actual sin and mortal sin.'

'Original sin is wiped out by holy Baptism. Actual sin is the sin committed voluntarily by those who have the use of reason. Actual sin is of two kinds: venial and mortal.'

We all repeated this in chorus.

'I don't understand,' said Baby.

'Oh shut up!'

Zeffirino said, 'The Devil was good too, once, but then he got bad so the Lord God cast him down from heaven.' And here Zeffirino pursed his lips to imitate the Devil's way of speaking and piped in a tiny, thin little voice, 'I'll go down all right, but you'll have to send me souls.'

'And what did the Madonna say?' Baby wanted to know.

'The Blessed Virgin wasn't there yet, what do you s'pose? She had to give birth to Our Lord, and the angel hadn't yet come down with the lily to bring to Our Blessed Lady.'

'Here's what happened: God created Adam and Eve, then the Devil came along to tempt them and said in a teeny weeny voice, "Eat the apple, Eve, eat the apple, Adam."'

'In such a tiny, high little voice?' Pasquetta could do the Devil's voice too. 'Like that, really like that?'

'Yes, it was, the priest did it like that too. They don't teach you much at home, do they! Don't they ever tell you about Adam and Eve and the Devil?'

'No.'

'The Devil's in the Villa, the priest said. And the Master will go to hell because he isn't baptized. You can be baptized when you're big, too, as long as you do it before you die.'

'And how do you do it?'

'With water on the head.'

'Why don't we baptize Uncle?'

'You're not a priest, that's why.'

'All we can do is pray fervently and have Masses said for him.'

'But my uncle isn't dead!' I cried.

'No, but we can do it to save his soul.'

'Yes, but Uncle is so good, don't you think Jesus will let him into heaven?'

'No,' said Pasquetta. 'Anyway even if Jesus wanted to there's always Satan who'll take him and scourge him.'

'Scourge him?'

'First he scourges him and then he puts him in the fire with the rest of the damned.'

'Real fire?'

'Of course, the priest said so!'

Baby began to cry again.

'And how does the priest know?' I demanded.

'Oh come, Penny. D'you think you know more than the priest? How d'you think the priests and bishops spend their time? Just listen to her . . .'

'I don't want Uncle put into the fire!' I began to sob. 'I don't want it, I don't want it.'

I began hitting Pasquetta.

[48]

'Stop it, will you?' she protested. 'Your uncle won't go to hell if we pray for his soul and make sacrifices.'

'The Jews haven't got a soul,' somebody objected.

'That's true, so we'll have to do penance,' they all said.

'Let's do penance,' said Lea, 'and the more we suffer the more it'll help.'

11

THE pen-nib scratched across the exercise-book.

Theme: We love Mussolini as our father.

Development: 'I love Benito Mussolini more than my father because my father is not here. I live with my uncle so I love Mussolini as my uncle.'

Then I asked the Signora to let me go to the toilet. In the toilet there was a lovely bouquet of flowers. Each of us had a little vase on our desk to put flowers into. The little vase would always fall over, with all the water, on to our exercise-books and ruin them. But the Signora's desire was to make a good impression on the Federal Commissioner* and nobody knew when he might arrive. He could arrive from one moment to the next. He might even now be at the foot of the stairs and coming up with the other gentlemen. When he came, it was always unexpected, and he was dressed in his Fascist uniform. They all would arrive in a car. The black car was all spattered with mud when he came to our school and once there was a puddle right in front of the car and the superintendent was angry because his shoes got dirty. One time we were all dressed as Little Daughters of Italy and the boys as Sons of the Wolf and we sang in chorus 'Fire of Vesta bursting forth from the

* Fascist Party official in charge of a province.

temple'. The teacher was brimming with emotion and she told us to sing and not to yell. We didn't yell but the superintendent put his hands to his ears as if to say we were making too much noise and there was also a woman, the Fiduciary* who passed us in review. She was dressed all in black and had gold braid on her shoulders.

'Step forward, you,' said the Federal Commissioner, but I didn't know whom he was speaking to, whether to me or Pasquetta, and besides I was afraid. So I didn't move. But then he began to shout, 'The fat-head on the right there! Step forward!'

When I heard fat-head I began to suspect it was me and I stepped forward and he told me I had tan shoes on. I'd told Marie and Elsa when they were dressing me to put on my black shoes, but Uncle came and said, 'There's nothing wrong with the tan ones.'

'Yes,' I told Uncle, 'but I'm a Little Daughter of Italy and want to be "squad captain" some day. And I want to have gold braid and march alongside the squad and set the pace.'

But Uncle said I was little and a daughter of Italy and that was enough and it wouldn't give him any pleasure for me to have gold braid and it would give him more pleasure if I stopped telling lies. And he told Cosimo to bring us to school.

The Commissioner said, 'Who are you?'

The teacher explained that I was the niece of the Master

* Fascist Party official in charge of the women of a civil district.

and then he made a nicer face and said, 'Give my regards to your uncle.'

The chauffeur came to fetch us and the children stood in the road waving until we couldn't see them because of the cloud of dust behind the car.

I brought my uncle the regards of the Fascist Commissioner.

12

YESTERDAY I did nothing wrong but today I tore my frock. So I ran to the kitchen to Elsa and asked her to sew it up quickly. Elsa sewed it up, but just when she had finished Uncle appeared and asked what I was doing in the kitchen.

I told him I'd been thirsty and I told a lie, but then he asked me whether I had broken the dining-room window-pane. I said it hadn't been me.

At table Marie wanted to know what had become of her ball of red wool, but before I had time to give Baby a kick, Baby said we two had taken it to play ball.

Uncle's face became serious. 'And where did you play ball?'

'Outside,' I said.

'I found the ball of wool in the dining-room,' said Marie crossly. 'I've told you over and over not to touch other people's belongings. And then why do you say you played out-of-doors?'

Annie began to laugh.

'But I meant to say indoors,' I explained.

'Then why did you say outdoors?'

'Because we pretended to be outdoors when we were in the dining-room.'

'All right but you were in the dining-room and the drawing-room, because the glass fish is broken too.'

'Yes but we were pretending to be in the garden.'

While Uncle scolded me and sent me to bed without supper I kept wondering why I was being scolded.

It's true, I admit, that the window-pane broke, and the glass fish as well. But are there window-panes in the woods? Are there glass fishes in the air? So what fault is it of mine if they get broken? We didn't do it on purpose, Baby and I. Baby had decided that the drawing-room was the garden and the dining-room the courtyard. Is it my fault if for Uncle the drawing-room is the drawing-room and the fish a fish?

For us two the fish was not a fish but an Englishman who was standing on a mountain top and whom we had to shoot, and then he died because the Little Daughters of Italy and the Balillas* captured the mountain.

It isn't true that I'm brainless and heartless. And anyhow it was the Duce who broke the fish because the Duce was fighting in the drawing-room too.

And then, what Annie's got to laugh about I simply don't know. The only thing I'm glad of is that Annie got a scolding from Uncle too because it's wrong to laugh at table when Uncle is angry.

Meanwhile I keep thinking of the day when Uncle will

* Fascist organization for little boys older than the Sons of the Wolf.

realize that I'm good and that my truth is true. I can just picture him coming towards me with outstretched arms to make peace and give me all the hugs and kisses he never does.

13

TODAY we went into the kitchen where Marie was making whipped cream cornets because it was Annie's birthday, but Marie chased us away, so then we went outside and played 'black corsair'.

I'm always the black corsair and Annie is always the black corsair's girl and puts on lipstick, and Baby is the black corsair's friend.

When Annie doesn't want to play, Baby and I, since we're just the two of us, are Don Quixote and Sancho Panza. The game consists of charging against windmills on our steed. I in front, Baby behind. I put a dish on my head, for a helmet, and we ride our St Bernard, Ali, with the broom in our hands.

It's Uncle who gave us *Don Quixote* for Christmas.

Then the other day Uncle gave us *The Headhunters* and all of us together took Signor Pit by assault. At first Signor Pit defended himself, but presently he stopped resisting, with his usual lofty air, and thought we were fooling. But I wasn't fooling in the least, and we tied him tightly, tightly to the trunk of a tree with the rope wound round and round him, and also he had lost his spectacles and couldn't see us, and couldn't run away.

It had been my idea to ask for a ransom, and I asked for all the sweets he had in his pockets and in his room.

But Uncle has punished me and hasn't spoken to me for days. What can I do to make him look at me again?

Some day I'll run away from this house where nobody ever gives me a hug or kiss. They'll all get on well without me and Elsa won't yell that I'm a nuisance in the kitchen or that she can't find the chicken (because I brought it to that poor stray dog Baby and I found) and Marie won't scold any longer because I told Leonardo she's in love with him. If I read it in her diary was I telling a lie? No, I told the truth and I was punished.

Annie won't get angry with me any more either because I won't be stealing her teddy-bear that I'm so fond of even if it's got an eye missing. I was the one who took it out, to give to Ginetta against the Evil Eye. Because they've laid a spell on Ginetta's sister Tosca and now she's stopped eating.

Baby, too, will be better off without me. But what will I do without Baby? On the other hand I'm stronger, I could survive on figs and grapes and then I could work and earn my own living and nobody would be able to tell me I was a thankless child.

Grown-ups think that children have no feelings and that I have no heart simply because yesterday when Uncle told me to go and fetch his glasses to read the letters, I dropped them in running and they broke. But don't I always dart off like a flash as soon as the grown-ups need something? Penny go and fetch your uncle's walking-stick, Penny run upstairs and get the chess set, Penny fetch the eyeglasses, Penny go and bring me my sun-hat. Even Annie thinks of me as her personal servant: Penny go and fetch the ninepins. And then they scold me. If only they knew the dark thoughts that pass through my head when they behave like that! They don't even know that I often think of suicide.

If I were to die, then everybody would be nice to me, and Aunt Katchen would bring me biscuits and Elsa a cup of broth and Uncle would let me come into his big bed between him and Aunt Katchen, and they'd hug me very tight, and I'd be blissfully happy and begin to cry.

So I wrote on a scrap of paper, 'I'm going to hang myself,' and I hanged myself, but as I didn't die, I hid, with the rope around my neck, way up in the skylight-gallery and from up there I could see them running to and fro, up and down the main staircase, in and out of the rooms, Uncle, Elsa, Baby, Annie and Marie who was crying and Signor Pit.

I've always thought Marie was like the Madonna; she's good and she loves me. But Elsa is bad: she said, 'That little wretch, she's up to one of her tricks again!' Baby didn't cry though because she knew I was in the skylight-gallery. I was sorry for Uncle and when he called me I felt like crying. But was it really true that he wanted me back?

I began to be afraid to go back without having hanged myself. I still had the rope about my neck but didn't know what to hang myself on to.

Aunt Katchen, in tears, began to call, 'Penny, come back!' And since she was crying, and so was Marie, while Uncle and all the others were outside shouting, even Signor Pit, I decided to come down.

My uncle looked me straight in the eye without saying a word. Aunt Katchen, weeping, asked 'Why did you do it?' Then clasping me in her arms she said, 'Aren't you happy here with us?'

Then I burst into tears and said I loved her and Uncle so much and I thought they didn't love me any more because I was naughty, and I said Uncle never took me in his arms, and I climbed on to his knee and my tears ran down his neck. Then he gave me a great fat hug, but right afterwards he punished me and sent me to bed without supper.

I love Uncle Wilhelm more than the Duce, more than Jesus Christ and more than Italy.

14

AT school we're going to do a play. We're all to take part in it. Elsa and Rosa are making the costumes. Baby will be dressed as an angel, and so will I. Marie and Aunt Katchen are making the wings. They're making them for me too, but Marie says I have too naughty a look in my eye to be an angel. The teacher has sent to ask whether Annie and Marie could play the violin and Baby and I sing a new Fascist song. Uncle finds the song horrible when we sing it and always leaves the drawing-room when Marie accompanies Annie on the piano while Annie plays the violin and we sing. Annie puts on so many airs because she can play the violin: if there's any question of going upstairs to fetch Aunty's glasses (she's always forgetting them), or if there's anything boring to be done, she says, 'You two go because I've got to practise the violin.' But then she doesn't practise it at all and goes out on her bicycle.

Baby and I have decided to smack her as hard as we can. But of course you can't very well be an angel with that kind of thought in your head. Serenella and Piera Cuccurullo make very good angels, though, with their hair loose over their shoulders. They're in the third form. My hair is short and dark. How I wish I, too, had long smooth hair!

Fabrizia, who is in the fourth form, will play the

Madonna, and behind her all the angels will sing in chorus. Several little girls will be seated on the benches. Others will have wreaths on their heads; I shall be in the second row on the right. I'll be wearing a wreath too, but Baby will be in the first row with a lily in her hand. At a sign from the teacher we'll begin to sing. The Superintendent will be there too, who is also the Commissioner of the Province. Annie, who is taller, will be dressed as a Little Daugher of Italy.

The chorus is rather complicated because it's what the angels sing and it goes higher and then still higher but I can't reach up there. The 'Ave Maria' will be sung when the Director gives the sign, then the Fascist hymn, and all the angels will rise and, transferring the lily to their left hand, will give the Roman salute. Marie too will be dressed like an ancient Roman matron holding a sheaf of wheat in her arms, to make an allegorical tableau representing the goddess Ceres and the riches of Italy.

15

Our maid Rosa makes love in the woods with Nello, while Pippone makes love with Beppa.

'What do they do when they make love?'

Zeffirino said that Pippone made love every evening behind the bushes and that if I wanted to go and see he'd bring me. Beppa is the wife of Cencetti who has five children and one of them is called Soapy because he feels so smooth.

'What do you do to make love?'

Zeffirino said you didn't have to do anything and that it was quite simple.

When we arrived at the top of the hill to look for Pippone the sun was setting. The tree-trunks were red on the side of the sunset and black on the other. I, too, had taken off my shoes and, by putting my ear to the ground like Zeffirino, could hear the sounds that came from farther off, on the other side of the broom thicket.

'Let's go and see.'

We went to the bush where they were making love. I saw that a man was stretched out on top of a woman, I could tell this because there were four feet and the head covered by the bushes.

'They must be dead, they're not moving.'

'Pippone has four legs!' cried Zeffirino and burst out

laughing but was cut short by a stone flung at his head. We began running down the hill. I had seen Pippone leap up from the bushes; he shouted and threw stones at us. Even now he was standing on the hilltop like a giant and hurling stones.

'Did you see?' asked Zeffirino, all red in the face, when we reached the bottom. 'They were kissing.'

In the courtyard there were Baby and Pasquetta and Lea and Pierino.

'We've seen Pippone and Beppa making love!'

'Really and truly?' they chorused.

'What do they do when they kiss?' asked Baby.

'They touch each other's tongue.'

'Pippone and Beppa touch each other's tongue?'

'Yes, they were touching each other's tongue,' said Zeffirino, 'I saw it with my own eyes.'

'They touch each other's tongue when they make love?'

Pierino said that those spots on the moon are two lovers kissing. 'Have you never seen on the moon what lovers do?'

'No,' said Baby.

'Then I'll show you . . .' Pierino stuck out his tongue and told Lea to stick hers out and they stood face to face and touched tongues. Lea jumped backward giggling and said that Pierino was tickling her nose.

'Me too! Me too!' cried Baby.

'Here you are . . .' said Pierino bending down to Baby's level. Pierino and Baby touched tongues and after that

[63]

Pasquetta and Lea touched tongues and then Zeffirino and I stood face to face to kiss. But then we all began making faces and kicking at each other and Pierino kissed me by licking my whole face and neck. Then Zeffirino began to lick my ears and we all fell down in the hay. The hay was full of lice.

'I'm full of lice,' bawled Zeffirino.

'Another kiss!'

'Wait till I catch you!'

The grain was nearly as high as all of Baby and we made an opening through the middle of it, laughing. Suddenly I saw Pierino's papa at the other end of the field shouting at us because we were trampling on the grain.

16

THE Fascist Commissioner came to the school celebration. Then Baby and I stepped forward and sang the song for the Duce. It went like this:

'Mussolini Mussolini, with cudgel and with cannon, with aspect bold and proud, Fascism and the Nation will triumph over all.'

Annie too, dressed as a Little Daughter of Italy, stepped forward, violin in hand. The teacher was deeply moved and all red in the face. Annie was red too and her hand trembled. She began to play but in her agitation forgot how to read the notes. So Baby and I sang at the tops of our voices so that the Commissioner wouldn't hear Annie play out of tune. But then we began to sing out of tune ourselves to follow Annie.

'Long live the Duce!' said the Signora when the Commissioner was about to leave.

'Hurrah!' shouted everybody at the tops of their voices.

But the Commissioner turned round again to question us. He called upon Zeffirino and asked him, 'Which is the longest river in Italy?'

Zeffirino thought it over for a moment, then Cesira prompted him: 'Po ... po ... po.'

'The motor-car,' said Zeffirino.

'The Po,' said the Commissioner, exasperated.

Then he turned to Cesira.

'What type of animal is the camel?'

The Signora smiled at Cesira to encourage her. She had, in fact, taught us that, and she had also had us write a composition on the camel.

But Cesira answered that the camel lives in the desert and that when he's hungry he eats his rump. Instead of saying that when he's hungry he eats his hump.

When we got home, Uncle gave us permission to stay dressed as angels.

Sunday there was to be the procession in honour of the Madonna. The peasants would carry her from the church in the village up to the Villa and then back again. They would walk with the Madonna on their shoulders making her bend forward every five steps. The women would sing 'Ave Maria'. It's true that when Pasquetta and Lea sing they do it so loudly that the priest always says they're screeching.

On Sunday the priest announced the visit of the Bishop to the village; Lea told me because we aren't sent to Mass. She said the Bishop would pay a call on our uncle at the Villa.

'The Bishop wears a ring that works miracles and one has to kiss his hand.'

[66]

'Then will the Bishop call himself at the Villa, specially to see Uncle?' asked Baby.

Lea said it was like the Holy Ghost coming into the house, and repeated that the Bishop has a great big ring which performs miracles. Baby said she did not want the Bishop to leave the Villa so as not to take his blessing away with him. She was busy arranging all her toys in a row for his blessing.

'How is it that the Bishop comes to call on Uncle if he isn't baptized?'

'Perhaps His Lordship the Bishop doesn't know.'

The Villa was all decked out for the occasion and gaily coloured rugs were hanging from the windows. Aunt Katchen and Marie were hurrying all over the place putting decorations in the windows. Uncle remained in his study, as usual, among his books. He was more on edge than usual and I had already been scolded. Everybody was running about and talking at the same time.

We children had been sent to the fields to gather flowers and to prepare a bright-coloured carpet at the foot of the broad stone steps where the procession would pause for a little and where they would set down the Madonna before carrying her away again.

A breeze lifted Baby's frock as she stooped to gather the flowers for the Madonna, disappearing among the poppies and the broom. Now and then her blonde curls would bob up and she would skip towards us, her small hands clutching little bunches of violets and cyclamen.

The peasants had written 'Ave Maria' in laurel leaves across the drive.

The empty spaces had to be filled in with flowers and this was left to us. The letter 'A' was all yellow with broom and the letter 'M' filled with violets and poppies. Elsa called us. 'Come at once and get dressed!'

She sent us back down the main staircase very clean with bows in our hair. Meanwhile the procession could be seen approaching up the hillside. The carabinieri were at the head of it, then came the priest, giving his blessing, then the acolytes, the Commissioner, the women singing and the children in white, among them Pasquetta. She seemed a different person, dressed in white like that. She was singing and did not even glance at us. Then . . . then . . . the Bishop; and then . . . the Madonna.

Beneath a canopy all of gold she was advancing slowly on the men's shoulders, bowing.

'Look at the Madonna, she's crying!' exclaimed Zeffirino.

'She smiled at us!' shouted Lea.

She was very slowly approaching the Villa. At the foot of the grand staircase stood my uncle dressed in white, with his white broad-brimmed hat.

'He could be a saint,' said Pasquetta looking at him.

'If the Madonna gives him the grace he will be.'

The trumpets blared and everybody sang still louder.

The Madonna made her final bow, then turned and started on her return journey, slowly disappearing at the end of the drive followed by the people.

'She waved her hand to me, did she to you?'

'No, not to me,' I said sadly.

17

MARIE was very busy. She was preparing the strawberries to be served to the Bishop. Marie was good at concocting the most unusual dishes. Today she had decided to whip the strawberries and make an iced sweet with them.

'Katchen are you ready?' asked Uncle in English. He spoke English most of the time and German when he was angry.

Uncle told me to call Aunt Katchen because it was late. Aunt Katchen sent me to the kitchen to see whether Marie was ready; while she was at it she took the occasion to thank me by pinching my nose and asking me several questions in English. The butler was walking up and down and making me nervous; he was looking at us loftily and behaving as though he were the head of the house. All the staff and the peasants were in the entrance-hall because they wanted to kiss the Bishop's hand.

The Bishop's car drew up. Out of it stepped the parish priest, a monk, another priest and the Bishop dressed in violet. The Bishop stepped out of the car, the parish priest led the way and Uncle came forward to greet him, holding out his hand.

In the entrance-hall the peasants and staff were waiting to kiss the Bishop's hand. Baby and Annie and I were there too. The Bishop seemed to tower above us and I thought I detected a wonderful light in his eye. Everybody fell at his feet and kissed his hand. He smiled benevolently and offered us the hand with the ring. The Bishop offered his hand to Baby. Baby clung to it and refused to let go. The Bishop jerked his hand, then shook his arm and frowned. Baby, clinging to his hand, sobbed, 'Save him, save him!' but nobody knew what she was talking about. The Bishop tried again to shake himself free of Baby. I saw Uncle come forward angrily.

'Baby!' he said in English. 'What are you doing!'

We all pulled Baby away from the Bishop's hand and he smiled again and entered the drawing-room with the others.

The Bishop's cloak was left outside in the entrance and the peasants kissed it.

'Stupid!' said Lea to Baby.

Baby sobbed that Uncle had not kissed the Bishop's ring so he would not be saved, and that she did not want the Bishop to leave the Villa without performing a miracle.

'As long as the Bishop is in the Villa,' said Pasquetta, dressed in white with the silk band on her head, 'the Holy Ghost will be here too,' and she nodded towards the Bishop's cloak hanging in the entrance.

I slipped into the garden and looked through the half-closed blinds into the drawing-room. I heard the parish priest ask Uncle why he did not send us to Mass, since we were baptized and our parents surely would have sent us.

To this Uncle replied rather coldly that he proposed to let us decide for ourselves when we were older and better able to understand.

And when the parish priest said it was not right not to go to Mass, the Bishop interrupted him and spoke of the goodness of God which is infinite and which sooner or later would throw light on everything. The Bishop spoke with great gentleness, like a saint.

Cosimo, the butler, came in with the strawberries.

I saw Baby running out of the entrance-hall and caught a glimpse of something violet in her hand exactly the shade of the Bishop's cloak.

'I've cut off a piece of his cloak!' cried Baby. 'So now the Holy Ghost won't be able to leave us,' and with the scissors she had in her other hand, she went to work digging a hole under the medlar tree.

'I'll bury it here,' she said.

That night Uncle sent us to bed without supper and I had to write for twenty pages, 'It is forbidden to cut up the clothing of bishops.'

18

THE bell rang for the end of school, and I ran down to fetch Baby who was getting Zeffirino to carry her satchel.

'Look!' said Baby and put out her tongue.

'Baby, look at *me*!' said Pierino putting out his.

'Which is longer?'

'Penny show me yours.'

I stuck mine out, but Zeffirino was the best because he could touch the tip of his nose.

'Come along young ladies, the car's waiting.'

On the way home there was a sound like thunder in the distance.

'Is it raining?' Baby asked the chauffeur.

'No, it's the cannon.'

I am very sad because the King put the Duce into prison and so his friend Hitler came and saved him, and now the Duce speaks on the radio against the traitors.

I no longer recognize his voice; it has changed, and he speaks of resisting, not of conquering. It makes me think of a different kind of speech at the Palazzo Venezia when the radio said 'Now the Duce is reviewing the troops; there he goes, the Duce is not walking, he is flying. Now the Duce has finished reviewing the troops and is marching proudly towards the Fascist dignitaries who surround him and can hardly keep pace with him. The Duce scarcely touches the ground, his glance is bold, he smiles and mounts the staircase; the officials have difficulty in keeping up with him, so brisk is his step. Here he is now, coming out on to the balcony and greeting the exultant crowds!'

Uncle was sitting in an armchair, looking depressed.

How well the Duce speaks! How his voice rings out! His speech was smothered at regular intervals by shouts:

'Because Fascist Italy . . .'

A roar.

'I say, Fascist Italy . . .'

A roar.

'Will not let herself be defeated. We shall conquer!'

A roar.

We roared too.

'Long live Italy!' yelled Annie in high excitement.

'Long live the Duce! Long live Italy!' shouted Baby and I.

'Shall we hang out the flag, Papa?' asked Annie.

Uncle did not reply.

Annie, vexed, turned to Marie and Aunt Katchen. 'The flag, Mamma!'

'Run along out of doors!' cried Uncle, looking very grave. 'You're making too much noise.'

We three ran across the square shouting and singing Fascist hymns at the tops of our voices. I wished the Duce could hear us and know that we were with him, that he could count on us, that we were proud to be Little Daughters of Italy and to give, if necessary, our blood for the cause of the Fascist Revolution.

At school, one time, the Commissioner told us that the Duce had liberated Italy from the Bolsheviks who wear red shirts, swear and always spit on the ground.

'Let's play War!'

'I'll be the General,' I said. 'Who are you?'

'I'm Fabio Fabrucci of the Third Infantry Regiment,' said Pierino.

'Thank you for your exploits, Captain. Did you find the enemy?'

'Yes sir, I found him and I encircled him from behind.'

'Did you? Without being seen?'

'Yes, General.'

'Where are the prisoners?'

'Here they are, General.'

They entered, with their hands above their heads, one by one. First Baby, then Zeffirino, Lea, Pasquetta and Angelo.

'Down with your hands,' said the General.

'Down with the English!' shouted Pierino.

'And now, Captain, give us an account of your heroic exploit.'

'It was like this, General. I was on guard duty when suddenly I saw the enemy. "Oho!" I said to myself, "here's the enemy".'

'How did you know it was the enemy?'

'The General told me so.'

'Don't you know that all the enemies have red shirts and are Bolsheviks?'

'Yes, General, and besides, they swear.'

'Did you tell them not to swear and not to spit on the floor?'

'Yes, sir, I told them not to swear.'

'Good, and after that what did you do?'

'After taking the enemy prisoner I took the Italian flag and planted it on the mountain top shouting, "Long live the Duce," sir.'

'Excellent.'

'Let's pin the medal on him.'

'All right, here's the medal.'

'Good morning, General,' said Zeffirino stepping forward.

'Who are you?'

'Private Alfiero Brissoni of the Sixth Infantry Regiment.'

'What do you want?'

'I entered the enemy camp unperceived and stole the chickens and hoisted the tricolour in place of the enemy flag. In escaping I killed the enemy commander with a bayonet thrust, his adjutant with a blow on the neck, all his soldiers with a little poison I had in my pocket and then I had a hand-to-hand struggle with the sentinel who wanted to sound the alarm. So I drove my bayonet into his heart and he collapsed murmuring, "Huuuff!". Then I turned and saw ten other enemies assaulting me from the rear and bang, bang, I laid them low. Then one fell down and made

[76]

as if to fire at me but all he could do was to tear out an eye, General. I gave it up gladly for my country.'

'All right, here's your medal.'

Pierino arrived. He advanced tottering on crutches.

'What are those?'

'Crutches, General.'

'What have you done?'

'Battle, sir.'

Pierino trembled as he spoke, his head quivering rhythmically.

'Are you wounded?'

'It doesn't matter, General.'

'You're a brave man, tell us how it happened.'

'I struck out right and left . . . heads falling everywhere . . .'

'How many dead?'

'None, General.'

'You're a brave man.'

'Me too! Me too!' shouted Baby, Annie, Zeffirino and the rest, some limping, some with their arms in a sling.

'You shut up!'

'I'm Trooper Fiorenzo Baccucci, Fifth Cavalry Regiment.'

'How did you lose your legs?'

'I'll tell you, General. It was dark and I couldn't see, and then I heard the voice of the enemy saying, "They're all swine, those Italians." So I said, "Swine yourselves!" And

[77]

I hurled myself upon them and killed them all. Then one of them said, "You're a valiant Italian swine." Then, without legs, I went as far as the window and hung out the tricolour. Then, still without legs, I came back here, General. Reporting for duty, sir.'

'All right, here's your medal.'

'Long live the Duce, down with the English. Forward, to the attack!' We advanced at a run, crying, 'Ta ta ta ta . . . Tarara tata . . .'

19

THE next day, after school, the chauffeur stopped the car at the side of the road. A group of Fascists were passing by, singing. They were dressed in black with stripes of gold braid and were wearing black boots and their lips hidden under moustaches.

'Come along now, young ladies,' said the chauffeur and put us into the car and brought us up to the Villa.

In the courtyard Pippone took Baby by the feet, threw her into the air and caught her again. Then he walked up and down with Baby and me under his arms as though we were two sacks.

Pippone said. 'My pockets are so big that two boats can go into them. One on the right side and one on the left.'

'Honestly?'

'Yes! Two boats,' he repeated.

'Annie, do you know that Pippone has two boats in his pockets?'

'Idiot.'

'Annie, let me have a ride on your bicycle.'

'You'll break it.'

'No, I won't! Annie let me have a ride on your bicycle.'

'You and Baby break everything.'

'Ask me anything you want and I'll do it,' I said, 'if you'll let me ride on your bicycle.'

Annie paused for a moment and thought. Then she said, 'If you make me Queen I'll let you have it.'

Since Pasquetta and Lea and Zeffirino and Pierino also wanted to ride on Annie's bicycle we made her Queen. We were all at Annie's coronation. How I hated Annie, sitting there on the throne, having her hair combed by Lea and ordering us to go down on our knees before her. We had become her slaves. Only Lea had wormed her way into the Queen's favour and become her counsellor.

'Skunk!' Pasquetta shouted at her.

'Skunk yourself!' replied Lea, thumping Pasquetta on the head.

'Enough!' said the Queen descending the steps of the throne. 'I want you to shout a hundred times, "Long live Annie!"'

We shouted 'Long live Annie!' a hundred times but it was not enough. We had to cover ourselves with earth, go down on our knees and do her every service she could think of. First and foremost we had to brush her hair. Then all my pine-cones passed into Annie's hands. Until one day I said to her, 'You can keep your bicycle to yourself.'

In fact we had discovered a new game: riding horseback on the wild pigs. The pigs were let loose in the morning by Pierino's mother and came back at night. During the day they roamed the woods and ate chestnuts. Lea says that when wild pigs find chestnuts, they open them without pricking their noses and eat what's inside. We're always eating chestnuts raw in the woods and then we get stomach-ache.

'Hi-i-i-i-i!' shouted Pierino leaping on to a passing pig. But most of the time they flung us off again, grunting. It's best to hold on by the tail or else by the ears. What fun to gallop through the woods, skimming the undergrowth and holding tight to their ears! The only trouble is that afterwards Baby and I stink.

One day Zeffirino arrived completely shorn.

'I had bugs,' he said, and hurled himself on to a pig. We followed him, shouting. Each of us on a different pig, squeezing our knees into them and beating them to make them go still faster.

20

We were studying the Ten Commandments and I wondered what 'fornicate' meant. Pasquetta said it meant, 'Don't speak ill of God.' Then I wasn't clear about, 'Thou shalt not desire the woman of another.' No such desire had ever entered my head. Besides I shouldn't know what to do with the woman of another. Whereas I had often desired a bicycle. But then I thought if my desire were really to be granted it might be a waste to ask for a bicycle; it might be better to ask for the woman of another.

Pasquetta has been confirmed. The Bishop tied the silk band round her head and now she thinks she's better than us because we haven't been confirmed.

'Everything's ready for Mass.'

'We'll say it for Uncle.'

We had made a church in the woods where Baby and I could also follow Mass on Sundays. We all knelt before the altar. We took, from a tin, bits of chocolate that we had resisted eating so as to save our uncle's soul, and placed them on the altar. Zeffirino brought some chicken. To increase our suffering we put little sharp pebbles under our knees for the whole of the time we said the Rosary. Pasquetta brought with her a statuette of the Madonna in a blue frock and a pink cloak and said she had tried licking the statuette and that it tasted of sugar . . . We all took a lick at the statuette that tasted of sugar. Beneath the statuette we had a photograph of Uncle and one of the Duce.

Lea said that Saint Teresa scourged herself daily at the foot of the Cross, and that St Francis slept on the ground even when he was ill, and when the friars said to him, 'St Francis, we want you to get better so you must sleep in the bed,' St Francis replied that he did not wish to sleep in the bed, and that he wished to sleep on the floor, and so he died. We decided that we too ought to mortify the flesh and sleep on the ground. Pierino went to look for a stick and returned with a reed whip.

'Scourge me,' he said.

Baby said, 'Scourge me too,' and she placed herself in position with her bottom up. She stopped her ears so as not to feel the pain. Pierino began to scourge the lot of us as we lay on the ground with our clothing pulled above our heads. He scourged us very solemnly. I received five lashes.

'Five, like the wounds of Our Lord Jesus Christ.'

'Do you repent?'

'Yes,' said Pasquetta.

Pierino began to scourge Pasquetta so hard that she turned on him and bit him.

Then Pierino handed the whip to Zeffirino.

'Do you repent?' cried Zeffirino, raising the whip. 'Yes,' said Baby.

[83]

'*One!*' cried Zeffirino coming down with the whip.

'Do you repent?'

'Yes.'

'*Two!*'

Baby, at the lash of the whip, cried out, 'Oh Holy Virgin!'

'Do you repent?' demanded Zeffirino of Baby.

'Yes.'

'And *three!* and *four!*'

'Ouch! Ouch!' Baby turned to look at her red bottom.

'Do you repent?' cried Zeffirino raising the whip.

'Yes,' said Baby, bending over again. 'Ouch! Ouch! Holy Virgin!'

Then Pierino took over the whip and began brandishing it left and right as though he wanted to kill the lot of us.

21

NELLO kept Rosa waiting at the crossroads and then did not come to meet her. That evening she cried because it was Sunday and she was all dressed up in her tight frock and the curls I had combed into her hair and the rose I had pinned on her bosom. She had done it for Nello. But Nello had stayed in the village pub playing cards with Pippone and the others and had said, 'Damn Mussolini!' I simply can't understand what Nello has against our Duce.

Ferruccio went and told the Party that Nello had said 'Damn the Duce.' But Rosa told everyone that Nello had said 'Long live Mussolini'; I don't believe it though, because I've heard him with my own ears speak ill of Mussolini and it has made me sad. If Mussolini had heard it what pain it would have caused him!

Ferruccio arrived at the Villa the next day in a black car and a lot of men got out dressed in black in the Fascist uniform, and took Nello, who was in the courtyard, and brought him into the woods.

But I don't love Mussolini any more because you've got to pardon your neighbour, and instead he sent for Nello and they came and took him into the woods. Lea says they gathered round him in a circle and thrashed him. Lea says you could hear the yells as far as her house, but her papa was afraid to go out. Rosa ran out of the house though, and into the woods shouting, 'Stop, stop!' but they caught hold of her and with great glee held her by the arms and stopped her mouth and made her watch them thrash Nello. Perhaps the Duce doesn't know about Ferruccio beating Nello up. So I've written him a letter:

'Dear Duce,
  I think I should tell you what happened to Nello, a friend of mine, who has had a terrible beating from Ferruccio because he says that Nello said, "Damn the Duce", but it isn't true because Nello always says, "Long live the Duce." I've heard him with my own ears and Ferruccio is jealous of Nello on account of Rosa, so please do something because I love you so much and I'm a Little Daughter of Italy, squad captain of the Rosa Maltoni school.

                                        'Penny and Baby.'

Uncle said we should give him the letter and he'd have it posted. But the Duce is so busy with the war that he hasn't had time to answer us, especially as the enemy is advancing.

22

ONE morning I decided to go and see the sunrise. Baby was asleep; so I tiptoed out alone and climbed into a tree. In the silence of dawn I could clearly hear the sound of the cannon, which seemed nearer than usual.

The sun was rising slowly on my right. I heard the sound of the various insects and followed the movements of a row of caterpillars who were crawling up the trunk of the tree in which I had taken up my post.

My knees had turned red from the sunrise. I'd never seen it before because at the Villa they wake us little ones at eight. I wondered whether the sun is yellow or whether it's yellow only for me. Does Uncle, who is a Jew, see it blue or green?

I made my lips round like Pierino and began to imitate the birds. By slightly shifting my weight from the right branch to the left I got into a state of balance without which, I think, neither the birds in the sky nor the fish in the sea could fly or swim. Holding on to a branch with my right hand, to the trunk with my left, and supporting myself with my feet as well, I found a position in which I could stay for quite a long time.

I began to count the leaves of the tree and when I had counted nearly all of them it was nearly noon. From where I was I could see the Villa and hear Baby calling me.

I heard a sound of brakes. A strange car painted with spots stopped at the foot of the stone staircase. A German soldier got out and opened the door for an officer. Then he stood at attention, making his heels click.

The officer ran up the steps and rang the bell. Ali barked. Elsa came and opened the door. Then Elsa disappeared and left the officer in the entrance with the door ajar. Soon she returned with Marie and I saw that they were talking: Marie can speak German. The officer stepped inside and Marie closed the door.

Since I was curious I got down from the tree and went over to the house.

'Penny what are you doing?'

'I want to look into the drawing-room.'

We held on to the thick wrought-iron gratings which were outside all the ground-floor windows. Hoisting myself up I saw the German officer quite alone in the drawing-room with the mirrors. When I was tired of holding on I jumped down and told Baby. Suddenly we heard the notes of a piano. Then the notes became louder and the Villa echoed with them.

'But that's the Beethoven sonata! The one Uncle plays!'

I climbed up the iron grating again and saw the German officer seated at the grand piano, playing. He played for a long time, nearly an hour and a half. He must have given orders to be called for, because the car returned and stopped at the foot of the stone staircase.

Marie said the officer had come to the Villa especially to ask to be allowed to play the piano, which he had heard from a distance. Uncle sent permission through the butler but forbade Marie and us to speak to the guest.

He returned the following day at the same hour. He was ushered into the drawing-room and left alone. The notes did not begin immediately. What could the officer be waiting for, to begin his concert? Marie, perhaps? After nearly half an hour he began. After an hour and a half the car came to fetch him. Before leaving, the officer, when he raised his eyes, could see us, and Marie with us, watching him from behind the half-closed shutters.

The officer returned the following day, five minutes late. Five minutes that seemed to me ages and ages. As though the Villa had fallen once more into silence. All the guests had left some time ago because of the war, and Baby and I, as we could no longer have fun over Signor Pit or Signora Edith and her paintings, concentrated on our new love. No longer able to love Leonardo, we set ourselves to loving Lieutenant Friedrich.

I found myself waiting for him as I used to wait for Leonardo. What a funny thing love is! I should never have thought I could be in love with Lieutenant Friedrich as I used to be with Leonardo. But what astonishes me even more is that Marie and Annie and Baby are in love with him too.

It's no use, women are all frivolous and light-minded as the parish priest says, and commit sins of adultery.

This time the officer had brought with him a bouquet of roses. He asked the butler whether it would be possible to see the 'schöne Fräulein' who had let him in.

Marie appeared, very shy, at the drawing-room door. She nodded and disappeared after thanking him for the flowers. Uncle had not given her permission to stay in the drawing-room. Uncle shut himself up more and more in his study among his books, and his face became gloomier and gloomier.

The officer returned a number of times. We watched him from the bushes but dared not speak to him because Uncle did not permit us to.

WHEN I went down to the stream I saw a great many soldiers bathing.

They had blue eyes and blond hair. How different they are from us! We Italians are too dark. It's fun having all these new neighbours round the Villa. There was lots of coming and going of cars and of soldiers.

To my joy and Baby's the soldiers even came all the way up to the house. So did the General.

The General sent a message to Uncle by his orderly, Heinz, saying that he was terribly sorry to disturb him but that unfortunately 'la guerre c'est la guerre', and he needed rooms.

Uncle shut himself into his study with his face gloomier than ever, after giving the General permission to occupy the guest rooms while the soldiers overran the barns and the olive-press.

The soldiers ran up and down the stairs and their boots made a great noise. The corridors echoed with shouts. It was the soldiers standing to attention.

On the dot of five Lieutenant Friedrich began, as usual, to play the piano. Suddenly—I could hardly believe my eyes—the General himself appeared in the doorway of the drawing-room.

'The General is sitting in an armchair listening . . .' I said, sliding down from the grille. Pierino climbed up in my place.

'The General is listening to the music . . . he's smoking a cigarette . . .'

'What's he doing now?'

'Now he's standing up, he's walking back and forth . . . now he's leaving.'

Our new guests, unlike the others, have so far been completely ignored by my uncle. Never does the butler enter the drawing-room to bring coffee to the General or to Lieutenant Friedrich, or an invitation to dinner. It's they, instead, who send messages to Uncle, for the most part messages of thanks for the use of the piano.

'If Uncle won't do anything about the General, let's *us* do something.'

'What?'

'Give me a minute to think.'

'You know Uncle doesn't want us to, and we're not to go into the officers' rooms and we're never to touch any machine-gun or anything without his permission.'

'D'you know what? If Uncle is mean to the guests it's up to us to do the honours of the house.'

'Penny is talking big, as usual.'

'Penny is talking sense.'

'Let's invite the General to dinner.'

The soldiers were all around the Villa getting out their mess-tins because it was nearly one o'clock. But we were at the top of the laurel-bordered drive putting some final touches to the magnificent banquet for the General. First there was a soup made by Pierino, and then there was the sweet. The soldiers were all around the Villa. More kept arriving with cannons and machine-guns. We were at the top of the drive with our dolls, playing at cooking. Pasquetta had lit a fire and was preparing soup with a little water, some earth, a few chopped pine-needles and leaves. Then suddenly the General's car arrived in a cloud of dust.

'The General!' said Pierino.

The General got out of the car. He was tall, heavily built, with silver tabs on his uniform and braid on his cap. It was hot, he seemed tired. He walked slowly along the drive and handed a number of papers to his orderly, Heinz, who stood at attention. It was very hot. The General took off his cap and mopped his forehead.

'We've got to do something.'

The General gave orders to the soldiers. He seemed worried and irritable. Even generals can sometimes get ruffled.

'General,' said Baby with a tug at his jacket. 'Dinner is served. Come, we've got it all ready for you.' And she pointed to the rest of us.

[93]

The General turned. We nodded our heads. Baby, her hands covered with earth, began pulling him by the arm. With a tired air he followed her, smiling.

'We've prepared dinner for you,' said Pasquetta.

'Thank you,' said the General. 'That's very kind of you.'

We brought the General to a clearing in the woods where there were large stones to sit on. On the other stones sat Fifi the doll, Tro-tro the yellow bear, then Pierino, Pasquetta and Zeffirino. Lea and I served the General. We showed him where to sit down and then we began to serve him. Baby tied the napkin around his neck.

'Here's a drop of soup, General,' said Lea with her face red and her eyes bright from blowing on the fire which was always on the verge of going out.

The General drank from the chipped cup and said:

'Excellent.'

'Will you have some more?' I asked.

'No thank you, that was just enough.'

'Now there's the sweet: it's made of a few chestnuts chopped up with a few pine kernels and wine.'

The General drank from the cup and ate off the laurel leaves.

'Are you comfortable?' asked Baby fanning him with a dried palm leaf.

'Perfectly,' the General told her.

[94]

It was all spoiled by the arrival of Heinz who stood at attention, shouting something in German, and carried off the General who thanked us and went away with his pockets full of shiny pebbles.

24

EVERYWHERE in the grounds of the Villa there were munitions and machine-guns. The General sent his orderly, with apologies for causing trouble, to say that he needed another room. Heinz saluted smartly and reported the matter to my uncle.

We were all at dinner. The butler and the parlourmaid were passing their trays round the faultlessly laid table. Even if there's a war on and the General is gradually taking possession of the whole Villa, our course of life is always the same. Uncle gets angry if the food is overcooked, if the flowers are not on the table, if the glasses are not the rock-crystal ones, if the floors are not well waxed, if Rosa isn't wearing her cap and starched white apron, if Cosimo, the butler, loses a button off his livery. The enormous crystal chandelier above the table must always be lighted, with no thought of economy.

'Do you always wash your neck?' I asked the General's orderly the following morning.

'Yes, every morning,' he replied.

'I don't, is it dirty?' I asked with the little German I knew from Aunt Katchen's lessons.

'No, it's clean.'

'What's your name?'

'Heinz.'

'Mine's Penny. I've got to wash some clothing for Poupée, my doll. I need the pump; does it take you very long to wash your neck?'

'No.'

'You've been doing it for half an hour.'

Heinz began to laugh, and to wash Poupée's clothing.

It was night. I heard a voice under the window calling 'Penny'. I looked out and saw that it was Heinz. He put a harmonica to his mouth and began softly playing 'Lili Marlene'. I had promised Heinz a big piece of cake for helping me to wash Poupée's clothing. I put on my slippers so as not to make any noise.

'Come,' I said to Heinz. 'But don't make a noise.'

I was afraid of Uncle's finding out. But Heinz was so nice, and his sky-blue eyes had lighted up with happiness. I took a piece of the cake out of the cake-bin and gave it to him. He sat down and looked at me. I poured wine for him too. One glass for him and one for me. Heinz finished the whole flask. I put it back where it belonged, then removed the crumbs from the marble table-top. I climbed on to his knees and took everything I found out of his pockets. There were photographs: Heinz's mother and father.

'Would you like some jam?'

'*Jawohl.*'

Heinz finished the whole jar.

'Now go away,' I said. Heinz pressed me to him and

[97]

kissed me on the forehead. When he hugged me the buttons of his uniform hurt me and also his ill-shaven beard scraped my cheek. 'Good-bye till tomorrow.' I pushed him out of the door.

'*Ja*,' he said smiling. He lifted me in the air and gave me a hug. Then he put me back again on the ground.

'Good-bye till tomorrow,' he said.

When I slipped back into bed Baby asked me where I'd been.

'With Heinz, giving him cake.'

I could hear the tune of 'Rosamunde' floating up from the courtyard. The noise of the crickets came in through the window together with the sound of Heinz's harmonica playing on and on until I fell asleep.

I love Heinz as I do Lieutenant Friedrich and Leonardo and when I'm big I want to have lots of husbands.

25

As soon as I awoke I thought what fun it was to have the Villa full of new faces and new guests. And I thought of Heinz and the General who had been working all through the night. I could hear Heinz's boots going up and down the stairs and stamping themselves to attention.

Baby and I would go out of our way to pass the General's room. One day, in order to see him, we arrived with brooms and said we had to sweep the room. I set to work dusting all the papers on the General's desk and Baby those in the boxes on the floor.

'Don't touch!' said the General and added, 'Boom!'

'Boom?' asked Baby.

'Boom, boom!' said the General.

'Boom!' said Heinz pointing to the boxes.

'Boom,' repeated Baby and set herself to dusting the General's jacket on the chair.

'I have a daughter like that,' said the General pointing to Baby.

'I brought you those,' said Baby pointing to the field-daisies on the General's table.

But Uncle forbade us to go into the right wing of the Villa or into the left wing where the soldiers were.

It was hot; the cicadas were making such a din that I

amused myself by stopping my ears to get a sensation of silence.

Heinz came into the dining-room. Rosa was serving breakfast. The General sent word to my uncle that he would very much enjoy a game of chess but that he had nobody to play with. Uncle sent back word to the General that he was 'at his service'. Then Heinz saluted again, clicking his heels together and bowing. Rosa burst out laughing:

'Why on earth do they have to make all that noise with their boots to speak two words!'

She began laughing so hard that she was unable to pour the coffee for Uncle, who rebuked her sharply. We were all terrified because Uncle was not laughing at all. He was looking very serious.

'Let's go away before Uncle begins to scold us too.'

Uncle frowned because in getting up I knocked a plate off the table.

'Penny, you will write a hundred times in your punishment notebook, "I must not break dishes." '

For me this punishment is terrible because it takes me the whole day to write such a sentence a hundred times.

The General was preceded by Heinz carrying the chessboard. He knocked at the door of our uncle's study. We two were extremely worried and wanted to see what would happen. Would Uncle play chess with the General? We followed the scene through the keyhole. Heinz went away after coming to attention two or three times. The General entered and Uncle motioned him to be seated. They sat opposite each other and Uncle pointed to the chessboard. They continued like that, in silence, for nearly half an hour, occasionally moving a pawn.

After an exhausting wait behind the door we saw Heinz return; he knocked, entered and said something in German. The General got up and followed Heinz after bowing slightly to Uncle. They had given up the game in the middle. As he was leaving, the General met Aunt Katchen who was just coming in, and kissed her hand.

'Can I finish the game?' I asked. 'Let's see what I'd do in the General's place.'

'Let's see,' said Uncle, amused.

'I'd take your knight.'

'Good,' said Uncle, 'and I'd take your king.'

26

It's quite a while, now, that Marie has given up cycling for riding. Always in trousers like a boy, she rides across country and returns to the Villa with her hair blown about and hands over Italo to the farm-boy to bring back to the stable. Sometimes Baby and I are allowed to trot up and down the drive on Lola. Often they put us together on the same saddle.

One day Marie came back and said they had taken Cencetti's oxen. Our uncle sent word to the General to give the oxen back to Cencetti and that it wasn't right to take them away.

The General gave orders to return the oxen.

Uncle sent word that it wasn't right to take away his fountain-pen, to which he was attached. Uncle also sent word to the General that it was not right for the soldiers to open cupboards and take things which did not belong to them. The General gave orders to touch absolutely nothing which did not belong to the army.

As it was Sunday there was Mass as usual in the chapel of the Villa. Baby and I slipped into the sacristy to say hello to the priest who asked us if we had prayed for our uncle's soul. I told him we had. Then he told us that this was not enough because not only was Uncle's soul in danger, but his body as well. In fact he said that Uncle was in danger because the Germans had decided to put all Jews in prison.

That is what the priest said. And since Uncle does not believe in Jesus, the priest says that the Germans wish to put him in prison.

The priest said that Uncle ought to flee and go into hiding because else the Germans will take him away, and that it's madness to stay here. I simply can't believe, though, that Heinz would wish to do any harm to Uncle, or the General either.

But the priest was so upset that he asked two or three times to speak to our uncle. It's odd because Uncle and the priest haven't spoken to each other for ages, not since Uncle refused to send us to Mass.

Uncle received him and we watched them through the keyhole.

The priest went away very sad because Uncle did not wish to flee. He talked a great deal to convince Uncle. He said, 'You are in danger, you must flee, it's folly to stay here.' But Uncle shook his head and kept saying the same thing over again: 'I've done no wrong, I've never done any harm to anybody, so why should I run away? I have nothing to fear. So why should I hide? Isn't that so, Katchen?' And he looked at our aunt who nodded her head and said, 'Yes, dear,' and cried.

Then the priest came to the Villa for the third time, and

went away saying to Pippone that Uncle was mad, and to us two to pray for him.

Pippone, too, came to the Villa to offer Uncle the hospitality of his cabin in the woods, but Uncle insisted that he had nothing to hide and nothing to fear. At that moment, to Pippone's great amazement, the General and Heinz arrived with the chessboard for a game with Uncle.

My uncle is right. My uncle always knows the truth. He is Truth and Justice in person and can never be wrong.

I studied the face of the German general while he played chess with Uncle. I tried to look deep into his eyes. But his eyes were so blue and clear that I couldn't see anything there but goodness.

'Are you good?' Baby asked him, looking him in the eye.

Uncle sent us to play in the garden. But I'm afraid. At night when cars arrive at the Villa I jump out of bed with my heart going 'bump, bump' and think they've come to take Uncle. I tiptoe out of my room and look down the stairs at the officers who come and go, clicking their heels and shouting orders.

I'm afraid. I don't know why. I know very well that Uncle is right and Aunt Katchen too, and that the General is good. But I'm afraid. What if Uncle's truth were not true? What is the truth? I should like the truth somehow to appear in large letters in the sky.

While Uncle, Aunty, Annie, Baby, Marie, Rosa, Cosimo

and Elsa sleep, the Germans work. Are they plotting against Uncle? I'm afraid. I hear boots.

It was Heinz: 'What were you doing there on tiptoe behind the pillar?'

'Heinz!' I threw my arms around his neck. 'Heinz, do you love us?'

'*Ja, ja, jawohl.*'

'All of us? Annie and Marie and Uncle too?'

Heinz carried me to bed and tucked me in.

'Does the General love Uncle too?'

'*Ja, ja. Gute Nacht.*'

Heinz went out closing the door very softly behind him. But I continued to be afraid.

A breeze was blowing and the curtains swelled out and began to flutter like ghosts.

27

OTHER soldiers had arrived at the Villa, and there were cannons and machine-guns in the courtyard.

'Don't you ever shoot?' I asked a soldier.

All the cannons passing along the road were heading north.

'Why don't you show us how they work?' said Baby touching a machine-gun.

It's annoying to have the guns right here and never see them fire. We hear only the rumble of the enemy guns which has become as continuous as the sound of the crickets.

It was dinner-time and Elsa called us. Marie came to table in her prettiest frock, with high heels and lipstick. This was something new for all of us.

Since the soldiers have come Marie insists on wearing a Sunday frock and high heels and on giving herself airs. She wears her hair up and sometimes she puts on lipstick too.

'What's the matter, why do you walk like that?'

She had begun swaying her hips like Rosa.

'Shut up, silly,' she told me, 'I've always walked like this.'

'Oh, pooh!' said Baby and began swaying her hips too.

'You're absolutely impossible!' cried Marie in a rage, throwing everything within reach at us. I wish she'd realize that when you throw a hairbrush at a person it can be jolly painful.

Annie began wiggling her bottom too, and then, when we went to bed, she took off nearly all her clothes and began to do a harem scene. Baby and I had to clap our hands and she, carried along by the rhythm, did a belly dance before the mirror.

'But don't you think I'm beautiful too?' asked Annie, and went on dancing. 'Well, don't you?' she asked again, resentfully.

The next morning we went into the woods to take all the heads off the grasshoppers and put them in a matchbox. In another matchbox we put the bodies and in another the wings. Then we went home and I looked into the drawing-room and saw Marie and Lieutenant Friedrich kissing!

If Uncle were to find out! And above all if Leonardo were to find out! I hid behind the velvet curtain under the large painting so as to see better. Marie was leaning against the piano and he came close to her and then . . . then he kissed her.

I went away. I feel sad. *I* want to marry Marie. One day I said to her, 'Marie don't be cross with me, I love you and if I were a man I'd marry you.' She seemed surprised. I'm sorry to think of a man coming along and taking possession of her heart. And what about me? Will Marie still have room for us children in her heart or will it be all taken up by her lieutenant?

'Would you marry me if I were a man?'

Marie burst out laughing. Then I made the same proposal to Baby who said 'yes' with enthusiasm and gave me a big jammy kiss. That's what they're like though, these older girls; as soon as a lieutenant comes along they forget all about you.

28

WE watched Uncle and the General play chess. Today the General asked Uncle if he were Jewish. Uncle said yes.

I'm afraid because I no longer know what is the truth. And I look at Uncle. But Uncle is smiling.

At lunch-time Uncle smiled at Aunt Katchen, whose eyes were red, and laid his hand on her shoulder. 'Will you go, dear, and see whether lunch is ready?'

Aunt Katchen went to the kitchen and soon afterwards Cosimo came out sounding the gong.

From the garden Annie and Baby dashed in to table and Marie left her red cardigan lying over the armchair and came in too.

My uncle pointed out to Cosimo that a gold button was missing from his jacket and that his white gloves were not entirely clean. He pointed out to Elsa that lunch was late and the rice overcooked, and to Rosa that the floor was not well waxed.

But since Uncle was smiling all my fears melted away.

That evening, too, Uncle smiled at dinner while the English were bombing the Villa. All of us were afraid, even Cosimo; in fact the tray was trembling in his hands and he said that those aeroplanes 'had it in for us'. But Uncle said no, that Cosimo was talking nonsense and that they were heading for Florence. However the whole house shook and the crystals of the chandelier were jangling.

Marie, Annie and Baby were white with fear, and Aunt Katchen looked at Uncle imploringly and asked him to let us go down to the cellar or to the olive-press. But Uncle pointed out that the room down below was completely taken up by soldiers and peasants.

Uncle smiled as though there were nothing to worry about and even made jokes, a thing he never does except at Christmas or on birthdays.

Heinz rushed in and drew the curtains tighter, shouting that the light was showing and the English aiming at the Villa. The Germans ran up and down the stairs increasing the confusion with their yells.

I held my breath when an aeroplane swooped directly over us. There was the sound of a machine-gun and directly afterwards a terrific noise like the end of the world.

'Serve the dessert,' said my uncle to Cosimo, and Cosimo served the dessert to all of us and the aeroplanes went away.

29

BABY came into my bed. First I heard her bare feet on the tiled floor, then I felt her weight on top of me and her breath against my ear: 'We haven't said our prayers for Uncle.'

'I'm just doing a special offering for Uncle.'

'What are you doing?'

'I'm lying with my arms stretched out in a cross, like Jesus, to suffer.'

'And how long will you stay that way?'

'Till I count a thousand.'

'I'll do it too.'

'But you don't know how to count.'

'I do, too.'

'Yes, but only on the ground, like St Barnabas.'

I dreamt about Jesus. Jesus was being scourged by the soldiers. But when He saw me He smiled like in my book when He smiles at the children.

'Look,' I said, 'I'm just going to Pilate to tell him not to let you be crucified.' Jesus smiled and said that it was too late.

Then I went to Pilate and said, 'Can't you see that they're going to kill Jesus Our Lord?' But he continued to wash his hands. I want to tell Pilate that he's a pig.

'No,' said Jesus, 'you mustn't say that to him.'

But I went to Pilate, who was dressed in green, and I said it to him and made a face at him too, but he just went on washing his hands. I began to scream but the soldiers came to take Jesus.

'No no! You can't kill Jesus Our Lord!'

And they took Him away and I clung to their clothing.

God the Father looked down from above without doing anything to help Jesus.

'They're going to murder Jesus, the Son of God!'

The angels floated up and down singing Hosanna with a lily in their right hand. Jesus was alone in the Garden of Olives.

'But why does nobody do anything?'

The angels descended in the form of three gentlemen. Perhaps they'll do something. The Devil was advancing on tiptoe. The soldiers were running up and down stairs with a great noise of boots. Jesus Christ was alone in the Garden of Olives and was weeping.

'But can't you see that Christ is weeping?' I said, and I ran to be with Him.

'Which is the way to the Garden of Olives, please?'

I went to Jesus and said, 'I want to die for you.'

'Thank you,' said Jesus, 'but now leave me alone because I want to speak to Satan.'

I went to call Satan and said to him, 'Jesus wants to speak to you.'

[112]

But he went on chasing the flies away with his tail. The sky was all black and there was not even a single star and everything was quiet as though nothing at all were the matter and everyone was standing about in the middle of the street.

'Can't you see that the Son of God is going to die?'

And I ran in search of help.

I met Baby.

'They're going to kill Jesus. Where is the Garden of Olives? Where are the Apostles?'

Baby said, 'I don't know.'

'Excuse me, sir,' I said to a man who was passing by and who was the janitor of our school: 'They're going to crucify Jesus.'

'Yes,' he said, 'I'm going there too, everybody's going.'

'But it isn't possible! He mustn't die!'

Then I went to Jesus and said to Him, 'Come away with Baby and me: there's a hiding-place in the woods.' But Jesus told me to fetch his best suit, the Sunday one. Then I went to the house and looked in the cupboard among all Uncle's clothes and finally I found Uncle's white suit and the broad-brimmed hat, but I saw Jesus coming surrounded by soldiers and there was Pilate too, dressed in green.

'Let me through,' I cried, 'I have to bring the suit to Jesus.'

'No,' he said, 'you're lying as usual.'

[113]

Then Pasquetta began to sing 'Hail, Holy Queen' and they all began singing, and Pilate too, and I looked up at the Cross and saw that Jesus had my uncle's face.

30

BUT I couldn't get back to sleep. I woke up Baby and Annie but they went on sleeping. I went to Marie and woke her up. I told her I'd had a bad dream, that I'd dreamed about my uncle, and that I was afraid. But she began to comfort me the way girls do when they're big and want to behave like mothers.

'We've got to do something,' I told Marie, but Marie said it was only a bad dream, that now it was over, and she turned on her lamp and explained to me that it came of indigestion and then sent me back to bed.

But I'm afraid. Is it possible that I'm the only one to be afraid? They're all asleep. Can't they feel the danger hovering like a gigantic monster over the Villa?

I could feel this danger, but it had no face. I could feel this enemy, but it had no voice. It was hidden somewhere inside the Villa, was crouched on the roof. I felt its breath, but was unable to see it. I got up on tiptoe and looked out through the transparent curtains.

It was hot. The moon was so round that it frightened me. From up there it could see the monster crouching over our roof. I had not the courage to lean out of the window for fear of catching a glimpse of the monster's tail.

I'm afraid. My hands are afraid, and my heart and my hair are all afraid too.

Why will nobody answer me? Why will nobody listen to me?

On tiptoe, with my heart in my mouth, I crept into Uncle's room.

'What is it?' asked Uncle.

Aunt Katchen said, 'Do you feel ill, Penny?'

'I'm afraid!'

And I burst into sobs, repeating that I was afraid.

'What are you afraid of?' my uncle asked.

On the spur of the moment I did not know what to say. I repeated, 'I'm afraid,' and stammered some broken phrases.

Aunt Katchen, thinking I had a stomach-ache, made me sit in the armchair and went downstairs to make some camomile tea.

Uncle put on his blue dressing-gown and asked me whether I had a pain in my tummy.

Then I said I was afraid because he did not believe in God nor in the Child Jesus and that his body and soul were in danger. But my uncle did not seem to understand, and as I didn't calm down he took me on his knees and I told him that the Germans would take him away and put him in a camp with all the people who weren't Christian and that the priest had told me so.

He began speaking to me gravely and telling me that he believed in something like human dignity but I didn't understand him very well and kept saying, 'Why don't you believe in Jesus?'

[116]

Then Uncle, seeing how hard I was crying, stood up and said that all right, from now on he would believe in the Child Jesus.

'And in the resurrection of the dead?' I asked.

'Yes, also in the resurrection of the dead.'

'And in Our Blessed Lady?'

'Yes.'

'But do you really believe?' I pressed him.

Just then Baby came in: she had been looking for me and not found me in bed.

I said, 'Do you believe in the Holy Ghost?'

'In the Holy Ghost,' repeated my uncle.

'And in the Holy Catholic Church?'

'And in the Holy Catholic Church.'

'And in the Communion of Saints?'

'Yes, yes, also in the Communion of Saints,' said Uncle.

'And in eternal life?' put in Baby.

'Yes, Baby, in eternal life. And it's just for that reason that we needn't be afraid of anything, need we? But we'll talk more tomorrow and you'll tell me about Jesus. And now go back to bed.'

Baby had clambered on to Uncle and was clinging to him, as to a tree.

31

TODAY the Villa has suddenly emptied. The General with all the soldiers, Heinz, Lieutenant Friedrich and the guns have left for the north.

On leaving, the General kissed Aunt Katchen's hand and asked whether he could be of any service to her in carrying letters north, since the postal service was no longer in operation.

I filled Heinz's pockets with the white bread that he's so fond of.

When the General's camouflaged car had left, my eyes were moist and there seemed a great void in the Villa.

Today Uncle's playing with us children because it's Baby's birthday. Today we can do whatever we like because it's Baby's birthday. In a few months it will be my birthday and then it will be my turn to make a wish that Uncle will have to grant.

The wish Baby's made is for Uncle to play with us. So today at the Villa there are only children and there aren't any grown people. We play blind-man's-buff in the garden. Uncle lets himself be blindfolded. There he is in his white broad-brimmed hat looking for us. We tug at his jacket and laugh. He's awfully funny! He doesn't see us and he can't catch us. Now he's caught Baby.

We change over to a different game. Hopscotch. Uncle's done it wrong, he's lost the game. We laugh. Annie and Marie laugh too. Today everybody has to play with us.

This time it's 'Grandmother's Footsteps'. We draw lots. It's Baby who's Grandmother. She's got to count one, two, three, slowly and then suddenly turn round. While she isn't looking we must creep up on her and try to touch her. Whoever touches her first becomes Grandmother, but if you're seen moving you have to go back to the starting line.

'One, two, three!'

Baby jumps round. We're all standing still: we've moved forward one step. Uncle too.

'One, two, three!'

Baby turns. Uncle, with a very long step, has nearly reached her, but he loses his balance, he's still moving a bit.

'I saw you!' shouts Baby, 'you've got to go back.'

'That's not so, I didn't move,' says Uncle, sulking.

'Yes you did, I saw you.'

Uncle goes back to the starting-point. This makes Baby burst out laughing.

After that we played hide-and-seek.

How funny Uncle was tiptoeing cautiously to look for us and never finding us, while we saw him right away, hidden behind the bushes, on account of his white hat.

[119]

'Caught you!' I shouted into his ear.

Oh, what a lovely day! I wish all days could be like this one.

Although they say there's no one like a real mamma and a real papa, I simply can't understand how I could ever love my mamma more than Aunt Katchen or my papa more than my uncle.

Aunt Katchen made Baby a doll out of an old dress of hers and said it was her rag mamma.

We were walking back towards the stream because Baby had forgotten her rag mamma there. Baby was crying. I hoped to find her by breathing deeply. Aunt Katchen had a particular perfume which had remained with the doll made of her clothing. I offered my doll to Baby.

'No, I don't want her, she's *your* mamma.'

'But if she's my mamma she's your mamma too!'

'That's not so,' said Baby bursting into tears. Then Aunt Katchen, not finding any more of the old dress, had to make her a new one out of the pale blue night-gown.

Baby went into the meadow with the new rag mamma under her arm and she kissed her and spoke to her and told her all kinds of things. She walked through the fields with her in her arms and now and then she stooped to pick a daisy and offer it to her. The rag mamma's long pale-blue train fluttered in the evening breeze.

I looked for a long time at Baby wandering like that through the meadow.

I felt very forlorn seeing that she had forgotten me and that all her love and kisses were for another.

I went away sad to mope in the medlar tree.

32

'THE Madonna has eaten it all up!' shouted Pasquetta.

She came running towards us, out of breath. She could run barefoot without hurting herself; and behind her ran Pierino and Zeffirino.

'She really has,' they said, 'she's eaten it all up!'

Could the Madonna have been hungry?

'Come and see!'

The Madonna had descended from heaven and had accepted our gifts and taken them back to heaven with her. We looked at the statuette of Our Blessed Lady that tasted of sugar. Baby asked why she had her foot on the snake.

'She's killing the Devil,' said Lea.

How beautiful the Madonna was, dressed like that in sky blue!

'Perhaps your mother is up there with her.'

'Really?' asked Baby.

'With the Holy Ghost, too.'

I looked at the little card showing Jesus holding in his hand a large heart surrounded with thorns. In that heart there must be all the sorrow of the world.

I looked at Jesus' face. How beautiful it was, with the blond hair and beard. I don't understand God very well, but Jesus I love and I'm sorry His stay on earth is already over.

'Is God the Father with my mother too?'

On the little card there was a white lamb.

'The lamb is Jesus,' said Pierino.

Then there was another card with a little girl who had taken her First Communion, and behind her was the Angel Gabriel who looked a bit like Jesus but without a beard.

'Each of us has the Angel Gabriel at his shoulder.'

I suddenly felt that the Angel Gabriel was behind me, and that he was just like me, but with wings.

'And what's this dove on his head?' asked Baby.

'The Holy Ghost.'

The Holy Ghost is the third person of the Trinity, Baby the fourth, I the fifth, Pierino the sixth, Lea the seventh, and Zeffirino the eighth person of the Trinity.

I told Annie that the Madonna had eaten everything up. She didn't believe it. So I decided that she ought to come and see for herself, but not tell anyone about it. I asked Pasquetta and the others whether Annie could come to one of our Masses. They said yes, but she'd have to confess first.

So Annie came and confessed. Her confession went on and on. What a lot of sins she had!

'You forgot to say about the time you put the salt in our soup,' said Baby.

'Yes.'

'And when you put a lizard in the bed.'

'Yes, and the time I ate your chocolate,' said Annie contritely.

[123]

'Oh, so it was you!'

Pierino decreed ten lashes on the bottom.

'Stop, stop!' yelled Annie, 'I've repented.'

'Do you want to pray, too, for Uncle's soul?' And I explained to her that Uncle was in danger.

'Yes,' said Annie.

'And for our Duce?'

'Yes, for the Duce too.'

'Kneel down.'

Annie knelt down and so did all of us and we prayed. We had pebbles under our knees to make us suffer more.

33

I THOUGHT I heard something rustling. Suddenly the leaves parted and a white hare appeared. But it fled as soon as it caught sight of us.

'It's the Madonna,' said Lea.

We looked after it in mute astonishment.

We hid among the bushes to see the Holy Ghost descend upon the Cross. He appeared in the form of a sparrow and, after pecking here and there at the biscuit crumbs, returned to heaven on the head of St John the Baptist and alighted on the hand of God. From there he flew on to the head of Jesus who sits on the right hand of God the Father Almighty.

One day the Devil came in the shape of a cock. He chased the sparrow away and pecked up everything there was. You could tell he was the Devil by his wicked expression.

'We ought to kill the Devil.'

The cock was still there and I felt I could see the evil in his eye. I'm afraid of the Devil taking possession of my body and soul.

With a yell Pierino pounced on the Devil, but the Devil had already slipped through his fingers. Pasquetta leapt upon the Devil but he did not want to die. We all attacked him with sticks and stones. Lea beat him so hard on the neck that it finally came off. We left him at the foot of the Cross and began to pray.

Then Pierino turned to us and said that Satan was not yet dead. He had risen to heaven and was hanging there, with his hands clutching the sky and he was about to fall, bringing a piece of it down with him.

'Truly?' asked Annie.

We had to raise our hands to hold it in place. Lea intoned a chant and we stood there with our arms raised and our faces flushed by the effort of holding up the sky. The sky is going to fall, the sky is falling; we raise our arms to support the sky. Satan is about to fall headlong into hell and then his name will be Lucifer. Here we stand with our arms stretched up and the sky is going to fall. We are red with exertion. Who will help us?

Satan is about to fall, he's falling; the Angel Gabriel with the fiery sword looks down from above and the angels sing Hosanna, Hosanna.

34

TOSCA, the village girl who helped with the washing at the Villa, was ill.

'Tosca is ill, she's possessed by spirits.'

'What nonsense.'

'No, no, it's true, she doesn't eat, she only wants to eat coal and ashes.'

Pierino and Lea said that Tosca was possessed and that a spell had been cast on her.

'A little old woman's done it, and when she wants to eat she can't because the little old woman says no, and shakes her head.'

'But where's the little old woman?'

'Only Tosca sees her, and then she begins to shout.'

'If the little old woman goes on saying no, Tosca will die.'

We went to see Tosca.

'She's ill,' they said, and wouldn't let us in. That evening at sundown the women came with black veils over their heads to say the Rosary.

One morning we waited for Evelina and Pietrone to leave the house, so as to go up and see Tosca.

Squatting there behind the bushes I felt very close to the earth and the ants.

'Look! The ants! That one's carrying a piece of grain.'

'It isn't grain,' said Lea squashing the ants one by one.

'You're hurting them,' said Baby.

'Ants don't feel,' said Lea, continuing to squash them one by one. 'We're so big, they don't see us.'

'Just think if a giant were up above us, squashing us with his thumb.'

'In heaven there aren't any giants, there's only God.'

'Just think if God were to squash us like that with His thumb.'

'He may squash you, but not me,' said Lea continuing to squash the ants.

'God hasn't got thumbs.'

'Not God, maybe, but the giants up in heaven have.'

'In heaven there's only God, stupid.'

'Stinker!' said Baby to Lea, sticking out her tongue at her.

'Do I stink?' Lea asked me, coming close, to let herself be smelled.

'No, you don't stink.'

'Yes you do,' said Baby.

'No I don't stink. Smell me, Penny, do I stink?'

'No, you don't.'

'Yes you do, you always stink of the stable,' said Baby.

'That's an odour, Baby, not a stink. Lea is right.'

We sniffed at one another. My frock was white with big crimson dots. Baby's was pink with little pale-blue flowers; it was transparent and you could see her embroidered petticoat. The bow on my hair was white, while Baby's was pink.

I wondered why the little old woman wanted to harm Tosca. Tosca's so pretty with her rosy cheeks, and always singing; now she's been lying in bed for a fortnight, with the little old woman beside her saying 'no'.

'Tosca! Tosca!' I whispered into her ear as soon as we got upstairs.

'Tosca! Tosca! Tosca!' said Baby standing up on her toes beside the big white bed.

'Tosca, do you hear us?'

'Here,' said Pierino putting a handful of blackberries on her mouth. But Tosca heard nothing and looked straight up at the ceiling with its wooden beams. Pierino's blackberries rolled on to the pillow, leaving black stains.

'Bring me the coal,' said Tosca. It seemed as though she were speaking to somebody.

'She's talking to the old woman.'

'Tosca!' shouted Baby standing on tiptoe and leaning over the bed.

It was a high, broad, painted iron bed. On the white wall there was the Madonna rising up into heaven and under her cloak were little men looking up into the sky. Suddenly Tosca began to yell and to twist herself about, biting the sheets as though she were struggling with somebody.

Terrified, we ran down the narrow stairs and out into the fields.

The wizard has told Ginetta, Tosca's sister, to kill a cock and take out its heart, then to catch a toad and have it pissed on. Beppe is an old man who wants to make love with Tosca and Tosca said no to him because she makes love with Brunetto. That's why Beppe has had the spell cast on her.

Then twenty pins will have to be stuck into the cock's heart and after that Tosca will get well. Ginetta, who is as pretty as Tosca, has to bring all these things to the wizard by moonlight and has asked us children, specially Zeffirino and Pierino, to bring her the cock's heart and the toad. Ginetta was crying. She took out a rosary made of little black beads for the 'Our Fathers' and little white beads for the 'Hail Marys' and promised it to Zeffirino for doing her this favour.

I have a rosary too. I always say two 'Hail Holy Queens' and two 'Our Fathers' for all my friends and relatives, for Mamma and Papa who are in heaven and for all the people I see in the streets and don't know. But I fall asleep half-way through. I always pray too for the Duce and for our Fatherland and for the Italian soldiers, that they won't lose even one little battle and that the English won't get here.

I made my rosary out of medlar stones. I want to become a saint.

Zeffirino came back with the cock's heart and the toad.

'Did you meet the little old woman?'

Zeffirino said that in the woods he had met the little old woman and she had tiny little eyes.

'So I looked at her with great big eyes like this . . . and then with tiny little eyes like this . . . but she just went on staring at me and seemed to shake her head . . .'

Ginetta was waiting for us at the crossroads; she was sitting under a tree and thinking we wouldn't come.

'Here's the whole lot.' He pulled out the toad. 'Here you are: the toad and the cock's heart.'

Ginetta took it all and gave us the rosary in exchange, and set out alone up the hill. She was on her way to the wizard.

The next day when we were all at table Elsa came in and asked my uncle whether he would speak to Pippone who was in the kitchen crying. Uncle sent for him.

'Master,' said Pippone taking off his hat and hesitating to come in. He slipped on the over-polished stone floor. 'If you can help us . . .' He kept turning his hat around in his hand. 'Tosca is very low, she's dying, Master if you could quickly send the car for the priest before it's too late . . .'

Our uncle sent Cosimo to fetch the priest in the car. The General had used the car but had left it behind and it still had some petrol. Cosimo returned with the priest all dressed as if to say Mass, with the white lace and the incense and the holy water and his hat on his head. There was also a server with him.

Cosimo told us afterwards that Tosca screamed when she saw the priest and threw everything at him that she could lay her hands on.

'She must have been possessed for sure, to throw things at the priest!' said Pasquetta.

Cosimo says it took four people to hold her down because she was writhing all over and beating her head and legs against the bars of the bed. The priest placed the crucifix on her breast while the others held her down and the spirits came out of her mouth howling and hissing and leapt out of the window. We were in the car at the foot of the hill listening.

The priest blessed her and when all the devils had come out of her mouth, Tosca stopped screaming. I'm a bit worried that those devils that went out of Tosca's mouth might come into mine or Baby's or Pasquetta's, or worst of all, into Uncle's.

The priest began to walk down the hill towards the car, stumbling in his black cassock.

'I've never been to confession,' said Baby.

'Goodness knows how many sins you must have on your head,' said the little boy who was server.

'Neither have I ever been to confession,' said I.

'God knows how many sins,' said the server. He told us his soul was white as snow because he had been to confession that morning and all his sins had disappeared. How I should like to wash my soul the way you wash your neck

[132]

and ears in the morning and feel all white with Jesus inside my body!

The chauffeur waited in silence inside the car. He hardly ever speaks to us. We don't feel at ease with him, Baby and I. The priest blessed Ginetta who disappeared into the house while he came down the hill towards us, with the crucifix in one hand and in the other his hat which had nearly blown away.

The priest said nothing. He got into the car and began to read his breviary.

35

The rumble of the guns had become so monotonous that the birds no longer flew out of the trees in fright.

'Shall we play Adam and Eve?'

'Who'll be the Devil?'

'Not me.'

But Pierino said we'd have to do the count, the one that went: 'Eeny meeny miny mo, catch a nigger by his toe, if he hollers let him go, eeny meeny miny mo', and it ended with Pasquetta.

'No, I won't be the Devil.'

'Oh yes you will.'

'That count wasn't fair. Pierino always makes it come out the way he likes and I won't be the Devil.'

'It was perfectly fair, that's the way it came out.' And he repeated the rhyme and again ended with his finger pointed at Pasquetta.

'No, I'm not going to be the Devil.'

Lea said, 'With a face like you're making you'll never be a saint.'

Pasquetta was about to jump on her, but she remembered that she had taken Communion and had Jesus inside her.

'Are we going to play or not?'

'We haven't got an apple.'

'Baby can run and fetch one.'

Baby pulled her frock with the little flowers over her head like a tent. She stayed like that with her head hidden in her frock, thinking we couldn't see her. But she was looking at us through the skirt.

'Come on, Baby, we're going to play Adam and Eve. You'll sing and I'll be the Angel Gabriel.'

'No,' said Baby with her frock pulled over her head.

'Leave her alone, the little goose.'

'Baby makes us waste all our time. She'll never be a saint.'

Baby uncovered her head and made a face.

'I'm tired of being the Devil,' said Pasquetta, perching in a tree. 'If you don't get started right away I'm going.'

And she went.

Then Zeffirino did the Devil's teeny weeny voice and offered me the apple, saying, 'Penny, do you want the apple?'

'Go 'way, wicked Devil, don't tempt me.'

Next the Devil turned to Pierino and said, 'Pierino, do you want the apple?'

'Go 'way, wicked Devil, lead me not into temptation.'

And so on.

'Baby, have this apple,' said Zeffirino in the Devil's teeny weeny voice, and to lead her into temptation he took a bite out of the apple.

'Go 'way, wicked Devil.'

[135]

'It's good!' said Zeffirino with his mouth full, coming close to her.

'But you're eating it all up!'

Zeffirino stopped chewing and was cross. 'Am I the Devil or am I not? I won't play any more, 'cause if I play the Devil so often I'll never be a saint.'

'Begone!' cried the angel with the scourge. 'Begone from the earthly Paradise!'

And we let ourselves be scourged for a long time because it's only through suffering that we can redeem the sins of others.

36

THE roar of the guns has grown louder. Baby and I climb into the tree every day to see, far off on the main road, the columns of soldiers moving north. They're like long rows of black ants.

Every day new detachments of Germans stop here and sleep in the lofts and bedrooms of the Villa; but the next day they move on. We can hear the squeals of the pigs and calves which they take and slaughter in the courtyard. At the sound of it Annie bursts into sobs, and then I comfort her and put my arm around her.

To stop her from hearing the cries of the animals we brought her down to the stream.

'Annie, don't cry.'

'I'm afraid,' sobbed Annie. 'They seem human cries.'

'Oh no,' said Baby. For a moment I thought the blood of the calves was going to flood the Villa and swallow it up.

'Annie, don't cry.' She stopped her ears with her fingers. How could I have hated Annie? 'Annie, I love you, do you know?'

Then Baby fell into the stream that passes beneath Pietro's house, where there are masses of elms and bamboo stalks.

I went to tell Marie that Baby had fallen into the water

and hurt herself. Then Elsa changed her clothes, scolding and saying we were naughty and that she did nothing but clean us up and that the Master wanted always to see us well washed and ironed and that we got dirty on purpose. In fact one day Baby had gone to Zeffirino's house and then had wanted to do pipi.

So Zeffirino brought her to the toilet and shut her in. Baby stayed there quite a while because the toilet was a round hole which emptied straight into the manure pit. Out of the hole came black beetles and all kinds of tiny animals which fascinated Baby. Suddenly we heard screams. Baby was no longer in the toilet: being so little she had fallen down the hole.

'Baby, what are you doing down there?' Everyone was rocking with laughter.

I was alone with Baby because the others had to help Pippone clean the cowshed.

'Good-for-nothings!' cried Pippone.

You could hear the sound of the blows Pasquetta was being given. Then some screams followed by more blows. We were used to it, we knew that for today there was nothing to be done and that we'd have to play by ourselves.

I went into the woods with Baby to gather mushrooms and wild asparagus.

In the distance you could hear the shouts of the soldiers up at the Villa. The sound of the birds blended with that of the guns which grew louder every day. We went to see whether the Madonna had come.

'Look! A sweet!' said Baby.

I bent over and saw that it really was a sweet. But as I looked I noticed another not far away.

'Another!'

'I saw it first!'

'Oh all right, I'll give it to you,' I said, having caught sight of still another.

'It's the miracle of the sweets!' said Baby.

Suddenly we heard a rustling sound. I looked up and saw a man with a beard sitting on a branch.

'Who are you? What's your name?'

'Joseph.'

'St Joseph!' cried Baby.

I looked at his beard.

'Are you St Joseph?' asked Baby.

St Joseph nodded.

'Are you still hungry?' asked Baby looking at the altar empty except for the bones of the chicken we had brought.

St Joseph nodded.

'We'll bring you something to eat,' said Baby.

'I'll bring you the pudding too.'

St Joseph swung down from the tree. He wanted to know about Uncle, where he was, what he was doing; he wanted to know how many Germans there were in the Villa, and the name of their commanding officer. He said he had come to save our uncle, that he wanted to speak to him.

Baby and I had our skirts full of cyclamens and mushrooms. St Joseph looked at Baby, then took her on his knee. He began stroking her curls and kissing her. He hugged her to him. I was sorry that St Joseph didn't kiss me too, and so I came forward.

'Me too,' I said.

Then St Joseph put me on his right knee and began kissing me too.

'Come back,' he said, when we went away to fetch something to eat.

'I knew that one day St Joseph would appear.'

'The Madonna of Lourdes didn't hug and kiss Bernadette, you know!'

'That's true.'

'But I'd like the blessed stigmata too, like St Francis.'

I thought I heard the gong. 'It's late, it's already suppertime.'

'We ought to thank Our Lady for sending St Joseph to us.'

Before going home we went to tell Zeffirino that St Joseph was hungry.

'Just you wait! I'll give you St Joseph!' shouted Zeffirino's papa tearing off his belt and chasing after him to get back the loaf of bread Zeffirino had taken. Baby and I stood behind a tree and listened.

But our uncle was sitting in an armchair and Elsa was very upset because nobody would come to supper.

'You've had us badly worried,' said Uncle. 'Tomorrow you won't go out.' We sat at the table and Rosa began to serve. When Uncle doesn't speak it's a sign that he's very angry.

I opened my mouth but Uncle told me to be quiet.

'St Joseph is hungry!' said Baby to Elsa when she locked us in by Uncle's orders.

'Is that so? Where is he then?'

'St Joseph is hungry in the woods beneath the big oak. He's come to save Uncle,' said Baby softly through the keyhole.

'The things they think up, these two! Soon we'll have the whole Holy Family to supper.'

'Don't blaspheme,' cried Baby with tears in her eyes.

Annie came in.

'Good night,' said Annie and got under the covers in her embroidered nightgown. 'Stop your chatter.'

We had put on our nightgowns over our dresses so as to be able to go out in the middle of the night when Annie was asleep. Baby cried as she sucked her sweets.

'Stop making a noise.'

'Noise,' said the parrot we'd been given in place of the magpie we'd killed with too much kindness.

'You don't let Pedro sleep either.'

'Pedro either.'

Baby and I began praying under our breath.

'Bzz ... bzz ... bzz ... bzz ... Amen,' said Pedro.

'Sssh! Be quiet!' Annie got up and turned on the light.

'Annie I've got to tell you something.'

'What?'

'Listen Annie, supposing I were to tell you that St Joseph is out under the big oak and that he's hungry?'

'He's hungry,' echoed Baby. 'Annie, would you give St Joseph something to eat 'cause he's hungry?'

'What are you talking about?'

'St Joseph is in the woods,' said Baby, 'waiting for Uncle.'

'That's a lie!'

'No, it's not a lie! He's come on Uncle's account; he's come to save him.'

'It's the truth!' I cried; 'It's the truth!' and I ran straight to Uncle to tell him so.

My uncle was listening to the wireless and seemed annoyed when we rushed into the drawing-room.

Baby told him about St Joseph who was in the woods, who had come to save him and was waiting for him under the big oak. Then Uncle said that he'd see to St Joseph himself, that he was sure he had come to save him and that he'd bring him something to eat, but that we mustn't say anything to anyone, it was a matter between St Joseph and himself.

'Since St Joseph is in the woods, as you say, I'd better go and see him.'

'And will you bring him something to eat?' asked Baby.

'Of course I will.'

The next morning my uncle said that he'd seen St Joseph.

'What did he say to you?' asked Baby.

'Not to tell anyone he'd been here.'

'I've always prayed for you. That's why he came.'

Uncle gave Baby a hug and told her not to stop praying.

Uncle looked out of the window at the wood where St Joseph was.

Just then there was an explosion very close by. Baby ran to the window.

'St Joseph will be afraid.'

'Saints are not afraid,' said my uncle.

THE roar of the guns has come very close, and the last lorry-loads of soldiers are leaving the Villa under the fire of the enemy artillery. The air is full of whistling. The bullets fall to the right and left like rain. Such excitement! We can't go into the garden because Uncle won't let us. Zeffirino and the others can't go out either, to come and play with us.

The main road is deserted too. For three days not a German soldier has been seen, not even a lorry on the road which was swarming with troops in retreat up to a short while ago.

All of a sudden the machine-gun fire and the roar of the cannons stopped. There was a great calm. After a little while the peasants began to come out of their houses shouting, 'The war is over! The Germans have left! Here come the partisans!'

We could see, at the bottom of the broad avenue, a group of men with beards and rifles.

Uncle went out and ran in their direction.

'Where is he going?' I asked Aunt Katchen.

But my aunt did not reply; instead, from behind the window-pane, she watched Uncle go off with the partisans and disappear into the woods.

My aunt hugged all three of us very hard and burst into tears.

'Are you crying?' Baby asked.

'Yes, I'm so happy.'

Then we broke loose and began to sing at the tops of our voices.

Suddenly there was the sound of a lorry.

'The English!' cried my aunt, dashing down the stairs.

A car stopped in front of the Villa. Directly after it a lorry drew up and about twenty soldiers jumped out.

'Heinz!' said Baby. But then she saw that they were dressed differently from Heinz. They wore braid on their caps and seemed all to be officers.

'*Hauch. Hauchauchauch!*' said two soldiers lifting us off our feet.

'Let me go,' cried Baby struggling to free herself.

'*Hauchauchauch!*' said the soldier holding on to me while I tried to slip out of his grip.

'Ouch, you're hurting me!' I said as he caught me again by my dress, tearing it.

'*Hauchauchauch!*' he screamed.

'Look what you've done!' I said showing him my torn frock. 'It's you who've torn it, now *you* can tell Elsa who tore my frock,' I yelled in a temper.

But the soldier, after looking puzzled for a moment, grabbed me again and kicked the dice we had been playing with, hurting Baby's hand so that she began to howl.

'*Hauchauchauch!*' said another soldier catching Baby.

'Leave go my sister at once, else I'll tell your Commanding Officer.'

I saw Marie, Annie and Aunt Katchen being pushed up the grand staircase by soldiers pointing guns at them.

'Marie, Aunt Katchen!'

They pushed us up the staircase of the Villa.

'Brutes,' said Baby.

'Ugly brute, I'll tell the General and Heinz!'

They shut us into a room and left a sentry on the inside.

'Look what you've done to my Tro-tro,' said Baby, stroking the yellow bear which she had picked up from the floor with a crushed snout.

'You've taken out his eye!' and she made a face at him.

Aunt Katchen called Baby to her. 'Be a good girl,' she said.

Presently an officer appeared and asked us where Uncle was. Not receiving a clear reply he left the room.

Then the officer came back and asked us the question again in various languages.

We said we didn't know and Baby said he had gone to St Joseph.

Marie asked the sentry whether Baby might go to the toilet. The sentry did not reply.

'I can't wait . . .' said Baby.

The sentry called another soldier who, with his tommy-gun pointed at Baby, took her out. The sentry opened the door for the soldier to bring Baby back.

We could hear bangs and shouts and roars of laughter; I heard the sound of the shattering glass, of the lamps and mirrors. One sharp blow and the piano was smashed.

'The piano!' said Marie.

Somebody was rolling through the corridors on roller-skates; the house was shaking under the impact of the blows and the boots. Somebody kicked Ali, who began to yelp.

'They're hurting Ali!' Baby dashed to the door but was pushed back.

'They're hurting Ali!' Annie began to cry.

Marie said, 'Don't cry.'

'Mamma,' said Annie, 'they're hurting Ali.'

Baby began hitting the sentry with her clenched fists; she hit him on the legs and said, 'Let me out!'

How many scoldings I've had from Uncle for breaking the big vase and the umbrella stand in the entrance-hall! I think of all the reprimands and of the thousands of pages these soldiers would have to fill in as a punishment if Uncle could see them.

I can tell perfectly which objects are being smashed by the noise they make when they fall, and by the part of the Villa the sound comes from. They're breaking the crystal glasses and the goblets one by one. You can hear roars of laughter at every crash.

What will Uncle say to the Commanding Officer when he gets back, about the crystal glasses and the pictures and his ruined books?

They came to fetch us and brought us down to the drawing-room to be questioned. Marie said it was not fair to treat us like this for no reason.

'Ah, but we shall hold a trial,' said the Commanding Officer.

The mirrors were all broken. Several soldiers were skating about on roller-skates shouting; our toys were all over the place. The yellow bear had been ripped open and stuck on to the top of a broomstick and was being used as a target. Baby insisted on picking up a ping-pong ball which had landed at her feet. The floor was covered with glass. A soldier, wearing a flowered scarf of Marie's, was running up and down the staircase looking for the ball. He saw it in Baby's hand. Baby held it out to him timidly. The white wall of the entrance-hall was covered with scrawls and you could hear bursts of laughter. A soldier came down the stairs in a woman's hat with a large brim. I recognized it. It was Aunt Katchen's, the one she wore on special occasions.

When they pushed us into the room I kept tripping over Uncle's books; the paintings were all gashed. It was nearly dark and behind a small table sat the Commanding Officer, on the left of the broken piano. It was dark but the soldiers brought lanterns.

The Commanding Officer smiled and bowed to Aunt Katchen.

'*Hyrhutyrhauh, jawohl,*' he said.

[148]

Then he translated it into French for us little ones, so that we too might understand.

The Commanding Officer was good; he had smiled at us. He would hold a real and proper trial, and it would be a mere formality. He said he was so sorry, and that he would question us one by one and then let us go at once.

Baby told the Commanding Officer about Ali and since the Commanding Officer did not understand, Marie explained to him in German what Baby wanted. The Commanding Officer smiled and gave an order that Ali should not be touched, and Annie said not to hurt Pedro, and the Commanding Officer smiled and gave an order not to touch Pedro. Then they again shut us into the room with the sentry.

The Commanding Officer said he would begin the trial, and smiled and said again that it was a formality. He sent first for Aunt Katchen, then a soldier entered and called Marie, and soon he came back and called Annie.

'Me too,' said Baby.

'Us too,' said I.

'Not those two, they're not Jews.'

And the sentry wouldn't let us out.

There was a shot and a scream, then another shot and another scream and still another shot.

Baby and I plunged down the stairs shouting. 'Marie! Aunt Katie! Annie!'

The soldiers were coming up the stairs. The drawing-room door was open. It was red in the light of the lantern. I thought I could see their feet lying on the ground.

The Commanding Officer stood in the doorway and would not let us in.

They shoved Baby and me outside. The peasants took us in their arms, away from the Villa, in the dark. I turned and saw flames rise up, and the whole Villa suddenly catch fire. They held us in their arms. Baby in the farm overseer's arms and I in Pippone's. From the Villa came sounds of wailing.

'They're burning, I hear them.'

'No, it's the Germans leaving,' said Pippone and put his enormous hand over my eyes. I strained my ears and heard the sound of the lorry moving off at top speed, and the sound of the brakes as it went down the hill.

'The Master!' yelled Pippone.

Our uncle was running through the fields towards the Villa; the peasants rushed towards him to stop him. Baby and I began to run too, calling:

'Uncle Wilhelm!'

Behind him a group of men, all armed, were coming down from the woods.

Uncle was running up the road towards the Villa and shouting. He was dressed all in white and seemed a ghost.

Behind him the partisans ran until they caught him up; then Uncle collapsed on the ground.

Uncle Wilhelm was crying and I looked far off at the headlights of the German lorry as it disappeared.

Uncle was still with us.

'Uncle Wilhelm, Uncle Wilhelm,' cried Baby, hugging and kissing him, and so did I, but he shouted that he wanted a pistol. He begged for a pistol to die with.

But the armed men with beards did not want to give it to him and then I saw Uncle cry like a baby.

'Why won't you give Uncle the pistol?' I cried.

'Give me the pistol,' said Baby to a bearded man, hitting him with her fists.

'Bad girls! You want to kill your uncle!' one of them shouted, bending towards us.

'Not me, I don't want to kill Uncle.'

Baby began crying and so did I and we threw our arms around Uncle, who was sitting on the ground and pressing us to him while he continued to ask for a pistol and to watch the flames; they were shooting upwards and illuminating everything as if it were day.

We stayed like that, Baby and I, beside Uncle Wilhelm, for hours and hours, watching the Villa burn.

'Leave me, I want to be alone,' he said to the peasants, who moved off very slowly. The armed men left in a car saying that they would catch the Germans and kill them.

They left one of their number as a guard for Uncle. 'Take care of him,' the chief called back.

Baby put a hand over Uncle's eyes so that he shouldn't

look. But Uncle trembled and continued to look at the flames.

'Don't cry,' said Baby, and hugged him. I hugged him too.

'No,' said Uncle. 'You see? I'm not crying any more.'

Baby fell asleep with her head on Uncle's knees, and I did too, leaning my head against him as he watched the Villa burn.

I dreamed I was roaming through empty corridors, past an infinity of wide-open doors which gave on to other rooms in which there was nobody. Nobody at all, and I was afraid.

At that moment I awoke. Uncle was no longer there.

IT was nearly dawn. The Villa was smoking. Baby and I went into the Villa. The shattered mirrors reflected the light of the sky, which entered through the rafters of the burnt roof.

They were there. And Uncle too.

Baby stooped over to look at Uncle, but she soiled her frock with blood.

'Are you asleep?' Baby asked Uncle.

She bent over Marie.

'Marie?' she said. 'Aunt Katchen?'

Baby was stooping over Uncle. She was speaking to him.

'He doesn't answer.'

'They don't answer . . .' and she began to cry and scream, wiping her eyes with her blood-soiled hands. Then I burst into tears and began to scream too.

At that moment the peasants came into the Villa and took us away.

39

'DEAR Baby and dear Penny,

Remember Katchen and Annie and Marie and me, and the things Katchen and I have taught you. Forgive me if I have been a bit tiresome, and occasionally gruff with you. A fat hug.

'Your Uncle Wilhelm.

'P.S. Do not wear mourning.'

When Pippone brought us this scrap of paper which they had found beside Uncle, Baby and I burst into tears. The peasants had washed their bodies. Vittorio had made the coffins out of the doors of the Villa. The women were praying and lamenting, saying:

'Jesus, Jesus, take them with you to heaven . . .'

'But the Master committed suicide and suicide is a sin, so he can't lie in the cemetery with our dead. His wife and daughters, that's different, they were baptized, but the Master, he didn't even believe in God and wasn't Christian or baptized . . .'

'He never went to Mass.'

'You can't bury the Master, there's no room for him in the cemetery, being a suicide . . .'

'We'd need the Bishop's permission . . .'

'That we would! And who's going to the Bishop, with all the shooting going on!'

'This isn't a fine coffin, poor Master, when you think he could've had the elegant kind with zinc inside and walnut outside, but I did my best, didn't I, young ladies?' and he turned to us; then Baby's weeping grew louder still and I put my arms around her.

At that moment the priest arrived, all out of breath. Baby clung to his cassock.

The peasants rose, weeping and wailing. An old woman said, 'And there's nought to be done, we can't have him lying there in the midst of all our dead.'

'Why not?' asked the priest, continuing to hug Baby and me to himself.

'Because he's not a Christian and he's a suicide . . .'

The priest looked thoughtful.

'We'd have to have the Bishop's permission,' they said.

Pierino and Zeffirino came in laden with flowers. They walked over the broken glass.

The priest put Baby down and said, 'Are the oxen harnessed?'

'Yes, Father,' replied Pippone.

'Then let's go.'

'Where to?'

'To the cemetery to bury them.'

'The Master too?'

'Yes, the Master too.'

The priest had the coffins loaded onto the cart, but the peasants refused to bury Uncle in the cemetery. Then the priest set out alone, leading the ox-cart down the hill.

The priest had already disappeared beyond the curve and could no longer be seen when Pippone started after him and all the men went down to the cemetery, and the women too, with Baby in their arms.

The priest was praying.

Baby came up to him: 'Will Uncle go to hell?'

'Hell is only for the wicked,' said the priest.

The peasants wanted to take us away, but they had to tear us from the grave by force.

'We're staying here,' cried Baby.

'Come,' said Elsa.

'We're going to stay here. We're going to stay with them,' I said clinging to the ground. And I began to scream.

40

BABY and I were in the cemetery. We were alone.

'Don't cry, Baby.'

'I won't cry any more if you don't.'

'Look I'm not crying any more.' And I dried my eyes.

Baby leaned over the grave and called, 'Annie? Marie?'
She put her ear to the ground.

Then she began crying again.

'They don't hear me!'

As she wept, Baby looked up and opened her eyes wide:
'Look at Don Quixote.'

Don Quixote de la Mancha stood before us in the gateway
of the cemetery.

Very very thin, very very tall, with a flat tin hat. His long,
bare legs protruded from short trousers.

Where was Sancho Panza?

Don Quixote was alone. He advanced as though he were
moving against the windmills, turning to look behind him
cautiously. He seemed rather surprised to see us. Then
Don Quixote smiled his own gentle smile.

'Hello!' he said, and advanced with his lance in his hand.
He had boughs on his head. He leaned over Baby with a
clanking noise and seemed to be breaking in two.

'Hello,' he said in English, 'any Germans around?'

His face was full of freckles.

'Hello,' said Baby, making a little curtsey and wiping away her tears.

Don Quixote brought his freckled face close to Baby's.

'Who are you?' he asked.

'I am Baby and this is my sister,' said Baby in English, making another curtsey.

Don Quixote looked at Baby and me, said something I did not understand, and pulled some sweets out of his pocket. Then, with his long legs, he walked off through the bushes.

He turned several times to wave to us. 'Bye bye!'

Baby began running down the path, falling down and picking herself up again.

10|63

DATE DUE

AUG 0 6 2009	

GAYLORD   PRINTED IN U.S.A.